The Comanche
Fights Again

Mitch Bayfield, or Broke as he prefers, is kidnapped and raised as a Comanche. When, many years later, he looks for his kin he finds himself unable to settle in either world and turns his back on them all. Because a young white girl who still lives with the Comanche band is still there, he is determined to go back for her.

After a bloody confrontation with the Comanche warriors, Broke and Little Bluestem are allowed to flee. But it's just a game. And they know that capture means torture and death. . . .

By the same author

Robbery in Savage Pass
Kato's Army
The Comanche's Revenge

The Comanche Fights Again

D.M. Harrison

A Black Horse Western

ROBERT HALE · LONDON

ISBN 978-0-7198-0815-9

Robert Hale Limited
Clerkenwell House
Clerkenwell Green
London EC1R 0HT

www.halebooks.com

Typeset by
Derek Doyle & Associates, Shaw Heath
Printed and bound in Great Britain by
CPI Antony Rowe, Chippenham and Eastbourne

CHAPTER ONE

Broke's arms stretched above him, his wrists tied with green rawhide to a low branch of a pine tree, and unable to touch the ground with his toes. Yet, beaten and bloodied, he refused to allow one cry of pain escape his lips.

His torturer, Black Horse, face painted with two black and red stripes across his forehead and chin, looked up at him, a puzzled expression on his face. He asked a question. 'Before I decide whether to light a fire beneath your feet, tell the real reason you came back?'

Black Horse waited for an answer. Broke unflinchingly held the young man's stare. The two men, when standing face to face, were of equal height although Broke was ten years older. He had known the Indian since the young warrior had been born. Now that same Indian threatened Broke with a painful death.

'I told you I came to get the girl, Little Bluestem,'

he said. 'I had to return for her.'

Broke recalled how he'd left the town of Hell, nigh on over a year ago, without any regrets. He'd headed for the mountains to live a life dictated by nothing but the seasons and the elements. He hunted for his food. Killed wild beasts with his bow and fished in the river with a spear. He travelled around using a small bullboat fashioned from buffalo skin and willow branches. His shelters were caves in winter and he used deadwood stacked against fallen trees to make a place to sleep in summer.

He enjoyed the freedom, his own company and was at peace with the world but for one thing. One morning, after a full year of living with nature, he decided he had one more thing left to do before he could feel completely at ease with his world. His friend, Little Bluestem, was still captive. He retraced his steps to the Comanche Reservation between the Washita and Red River, the land that was to the east of the Lazy Z Ranch, near the Goodnight-Loving cattle trail to find her.

No one stopped him entering the reservation but everyone watched as he approached the leaders of the Comanche. He did not bow his head before the warrior Fighting Bear who stood his twin sons, Black Horse and Wolf Slayer. He spoke as an equal. They listened as he stated his business, but their eyes were cold. Black Horse spat at the ground as Broke

6

described himself as a friend and brother of the Comanche. Over the years Broke had earned the respect of Comanche people. He'd hoped that would be enough to achieve Little Bluestem's release.

The twins, now sixteen, had enough status to convince the other braves that Broke was the Comanche's enemy. And now he was in a lot of trouble.

There was a history between the three men, especially Broke and Black Horse. They'd been brought up as brothers, though Broke had been near his tenth year when the twins, Black Horse and Wolf Slayer were born. Beautiful Woman, their mother, had held Broke in high esteem. Until Broke had been brought to the camp, she'd been known as the Barren Woman. His arrival, she said, had blessed her union with the great warrior Fighting Bear. When he left the Comanche band, after the death of Beautiful Woman to seek his own family, Black Horse had seen it as a betrayal.

Broke knew the young Indian resented his interference in Comanche affairs. When they had kidnapped a white boy, Broke had returned to the band and asked for the child's release. He challenged their belief that it was right to keep slaves. When told the boy wouldn't be a slave, but brought up as one of their own, Broke had asked if he could take a young Comanche and bring him up as Paleface.

7

Broke had won the boy's freedom.

True, he hadn't dishonoured the Comanche because he'd helped the younger warriors gain status by counting coup on a group of high status towns-folk. It was easy to kill, but to get near enough to your enemy to strike him and draw back unscathed – that was a great accomplishment. Broke convinced all the important people in his town it was a good idea. They'd stood together and the Comanche braves had touched each one of them.

However, afterwards Black Horse made it plain that his feeling had changed. Broke expected too much. He was no longer one of the group.

The resentment he felt then had resurfaced when Broke came back to ask for Little Bluestem's release.

Broke's wrists ached with the green rawhide around them. It was an exquisite form of agony as the leather shrank and tightened and ate into his flesh.

'You suffer all this for a lowly squaw?'

'Why do you torture me if she is so unimportant? A man who makes so much fuss about a woman must surely be weak.'

The knife slashed across Broke's naked muscular chest, which gleamed with sweat, to add to the zigzag pattern Black Horse had started many hours ago. Broke gritted his teeth.

'We will find out who is weak. You might think pain is fleeting, but I have lots of time to teach you that it's not,' Black Horse said. He watched the blood flow out quickly and then slowly clot on Broke's belly above the breechcloth he wore. 'Do you expect us to be generous again because we allowed the Paleface boy to go free? It doesn't give you the right to come here and bargain for anyone you want.'

'No. It's not because I think I have a right to interfere in your ways,' Broke said. 'This time I came to ask your father, Fighting Bear, to let me take Little Bluestem.' Broke felt another slash of the knife. His body jerked with the force but he didn't cry out. Again he told his tormentor why he was here. 'I want to take her to her own people. She has the right to live with them if she chooses.'

'She has no rights. And neither do you,' Black Horse said. The scowl across his painted face told everyone he wasn't convinced Broke's motives were honourable. In his experience the Palefaces had strewn the plains with their broken promises like seeds. 'You left our band of warriors. You belong to the Palefaces. They are the enemies who have reneged on the treaties, taken our lands and forced us into reservations.'

'I have nothing to do with that,' Broke said.

'You're a Paleface.'

'Thanks to you I am neither a Paleface nor a Comanche. I live in no-man's land.'

Black Horse's knife came down again and Broke said nothing else.

'Drink this.'

Broke looked up into Little Bluestem's eyes, as blue as his own, and tried to smile. He hadn't been released from his bondage; he still hung from the branch of the tree. She'd climbed the trunk of the pine tree and crawled along the branch to reach him. It proved no problem at all, with her slim, athletic build, to reach over to him. Broke's smile turned into a grimace as the skin on his top lip split. He gratefully licked at the drops of water that wetted his lips and opened his mouth for more.

'Black Horse has turned into a monster. I can't understand the evil that lurks inside him,' she said. Her blonde hair, darkened by bear grease, was worn in plaits. Despite the severe style, a fuzz of curls escaped and framed her face. Older women cut their hair short but she was considered a child. It was no child who held a knife in her hand, but, unlike Black Horse, she wasn't going to use it to torture Broke. 'I'll cut you down. Everyone is sleeping. When you passed out they decided to have their feast. They won't be back for a while. But they will be back. Take the chance to run.'

Broke mouthed the word, 'No.'

'Please,' she said. 'They'll take pleasure in watching you die.'

Although the Comanche tortured people to the

death they also thought of it as a rite of passage. If a man were fearless enough to withstand the treatment he could be released with honour. Broke wanted to take Little Bluestem with him. If he ran away he might be caught with the young woman in tow but to leave her would be unthinkable. She, like him, was white.

He saw the girl shake her head, her eyes filled not only with understanding, but also regret. She gave him a little more water; wise enough to know that he might be sick if she gave him too much. He'd not eaten for many days and his stomach wouldn't take kindly to filling too quickly.

'I have something I can give you later if you cannot take anymore. It will make the passing into the next world easier to bear. I have learnt this from the medicine man. No one notices a young girl who sits quietly making baskets or grinding corn.'

He smiled at her and, from the blank look of his eyes, she knew instinctively that he would refuse the offer of datura. He spoke through cracked lips, 'You must escape yourself if I die. They might turn their anger towards you. Go now before anyone sees you.'

She climbed down the tree and Broke watched the long-legged girl lope away, until she disappeared from view.

The warning for Little Bluestem came too late. Someone else had seen the young man and girl. The once revered warrior, Fighting Bear, watched the two and his face filled with sadness. He didn't want to see the twins, Black Horse and Wolf Slayer, hurting their brother like this. And that is what the men were, brothers, though Broke was able to count at least twenty-five summers, and the twins sixteen. They were old enough in Comanche terms to become fully-fledged warriors. Fighting Bear, now given the status as an elder in the Comanche band, doubted it would be possible to make Broke beg for mercy and prayed the young man wouldn't die before he was released with honour.

Unlike his twin sons, Fighting Bear held the man, who was his adopted son, in esteem and affection. He'd gained his Comanche name 'Broke' only because he'd been injured whilst being taken from his home. The only word uttered was 'Broke' when his leg was nearly severed. He withstood the ministrations of the women who'd sewn the flesh wound, and the medicine man who'd chanted and anointed it with magic potions. This, together with his courage as a boy, had given Broke status.

Fighting Bear's lined, weather-beaten face puckered with concern. He wanted to help Broke and after thinking about it for a while he decided it was the duty of older people to bring their wisdom to the situation.

He called a meeting of the other elders to discuss what they could do. They sat in the teepee, its opening facing east to greet the rising sun and the new day, and smoked. The calumet they passed around the circle was the one that Broke had given Fighting Bear as a present. The feel of the intricately worked pipe in his hands brought back memories of the time the boy lived with them as a Comanche.

Although there was a lot of bad feeling when he left, many of the Comanche thought it was the right time because he had grown and his boyhood was behind him. He needed to find his people again. When he'd returned to visit and ask a favour, Broke had not told Fighting Bear what had happened between his father and brothers but he guessed that it had not gone well.

Fighting Bear believed Broke's mistake was to come back again to try and take Little Bluestem with him. The young white girl would soon be reaching womanhood. Black Horse had told his father recently he was ready to take her as a bride.

And that was the problem: Broke wanted her as well. He wanted to take her back to her people.

Black Horse wanted her to stay.

CHAPTER TWO

As Fighting Bear sat by the fire in the teepee he put a question to the other elders. Outside, unaware of the meeting, the younger Comanche slept off the effects of the feast, and the firewater.

'Has Black Horse allowed his heart to rule his head?' Fighting Bear asked.

It wasn't something he asked lightly. There would be consequences to the question. Black Horse desperately wanted to become a leader. He had completed many tasks and one that had given him great status had been provided by the very person he was now torturing.

The elders refrained from commenting immediately. They passed the pipe around again to give them time to think. They would make no criticism of the youngster's behaviour if what he did were based on common sense. However Fighting Bear's accusation concerned them.

The One Who Tracked Buffalo passed the pipe along and then spoke to the circle of men. 'How can we trust Black Horse to make decisions in our community if he allows his emotions to overcome him?'

Others nodded in agreement.

Green Hat touched his prized coloured Stetson for good luck before he spoke, 'Black Horse shouldn't be taking a Paleface for his woman.'

'That isn't what this meeting is about,' Dull Knife said. He had no respect for an Indian who wore a paleface's hat, whether it was green or not.

'Why didn't he fight for her?' Calling to Animals asked.

'I don't know. It's too late for that because Broke is so weak. It would not be a fair fight,' Fighting Bear said.

'It would never have been fair. He's had ten summers longer on this earth than Black Horse.'

'We could've have taken that into account and tied one arm to his side,' The One Who Tracked Buffalo said.

'I think we ought to punish Black Horse for his actions.'

'Our people need to be told about it,' Green Hat said.

Others agreed and a crescendo of noise filled the teepee. Fighting Bear held up his hands to bring the discussion to an end.

'It is a grave mistake, I agree. But the youngsters

have become harder to control since the move to the reservation. We are less respected and need to be aware of this.'

'So what shall we do? Ignore his poor judgement?' Green Hat asked.

'That, from someone who wears a hat with mould all over it!' Dull Knife guffawed.

Green Hat was not happy with the comment but shrugged his shoulders and smiled. It was well known that Dull Knife coveted things he could not have. And Green Hat pulled the Stetson firmly on to his head to underline this.

The elders couldn't agree and for a moment Fighting Bear felt as if he'd made a mistake to bring it to their attention. But then an idea came to him.

'I will speak to the boy.' He explained his plan to them. 'It will give him a chance to redeem himself . . . if not I will abide by your decision to make our displeasure with him known to everyone.'

When Black Horse woke from his slumbers he was told by one of the squaws that his father wished to speak to him. An hour after the discussion between the elders, Fighting Bear and his eldest son stood face to face outside the teepee. It wasn't an easy meeting. As Black Horse and his brother Wolf Slayer grew into adults, the arguments between them and their father, Fighting Bear, had increased. The boys had been brought up to compete and gain prestige through their prowess as fighters but now the old men had accepted a place on a reservation. They lost status as warriors in the eyes of the young Comanche. To them there was no other reason for existence but to fight.

Fighting Bear, in turn, found it difficult to accept that his standing in the band was losing importance. He still dictated to his sons. As he bargained for peace between Black Horse and Broke, he failed to notice his son clenching and unclenching his fists.

Fighting Bear could never imagine one of his sons raising a hand to his father. They owed him too much.

As young boys they'd heard the story of how their father, proud of the two sons his wife had borne, had refused to allow them to be killed. Two children born at once were considered abominations. Beautiful Mother had begged for her husband's help to stop what was normal practice with twins. Fighting Bear's argument, that his wife had been barren for such a long time that her body naturally produced two children instead of one, influenced few to allow the boys to live. But they were swayed by the suggestion of an idea acceptable to their culture. They all held strength of character and body with high regard. If the children survived a night out in the wilderness alone they had earned the right to stay amongst them.

The knowledge of this story, of how his father had succeeded in bargaining for their lives, stayed Black

Horse's hand but not his tongue.

'Broke may have lived with us for a long time but he is not Comanche now. He chose to leave us. He cannot come back and demand Little Bluestem. I want her.'

'Heed my words, Black Horse,' Fighting Bear said. 'Broke is a brave man who shows no fear. He is like a brother. To kill him will bring his spirit seeking revenge. His magic might be too powerful to control.'

The Comanche's sacrosanct taboo against killing one's own people made Black Horse hesitate. Then he said, 'I will let Broke go, but only so I can give chase and kill him away from your eyes. Old man, your time is over. They say the brave die young. What does that say about you?'

Fighting Bear, a legend for his prowess in killing cave bears, refused to hang his head in shame. He had lived many years and contributed more than anyone to heap honour on the Comanche.

'You are a brave, fearless warrior, my son. In a few years you may be a leader and I may have passed on to the spirit world. I hope somewhere in that intervening time you will find wisdom and common sense.'

Black Horse went back to the other braves after speaking with his father. He was angry yet the words had affected him greatly. He didn't want to incur the wrath of evil spirits. Nevertheless he didn't want to lose face. He went to Broke and described what else he might do. He pulled off the breechcloth that covered Broke's loins and left him naked.

'You will never have the pride of a father,' he said. He made ugly gestures that everyone could understand. 'I will remove that part of you with hot irons – see, they are heating them over the flames.' Broke showed no emotion. 'I have heard men scream until their voices have gone. They've begged to their god to take them from this earth. But He never listens. They have to wait until I've pulled them apart bit by bit. Sometimes the women help me as well.'

Broke stared at Black Horse and the braves who waited for him to beg for mercy after the torture had been described to him. To their amazement he laughed and scorned his Comanche brother.

'You have to ask the women to help you?'

Black Horse lifted his tomahawk to strike him but Fighting Bear's warning was on his mind and he lowered it again. He could not kill him here.

'I see you are either brave, or foolhardy,' he said. He turned to his brother to consult him and saw Fighting Bear, standing by his teepee. His father's face mirrored his own primeval fear of killing a brother. He knew he had to let him go and hoped Wolf Slayer would agree. 'Do you think we ought to give him a chance to prove his bravery?'

The others waited to see what Wolf Slayer would answer.

'I agree with you, Black Horse.' He held up his hand when the other braves started to protest. 'We will chase him. And if he gets as far as the Rocky Mountains, then we will allow him to go free.'

CHAPTER THREE

Marshal Jones kept to his office and prayed for someone brave, or foolish enough, to take over his job. He knew his deputy, Don Wills, drooled at the thought of stepping into his marshal's boots. He wanted to wear a shiny big badge and a ten-gallon hat, but his brains were so small they wouldn't fill a canary's bowl let alone a Stetson.

However he held that there would be few takers to maintain law and order in Hell. It was an unfortunate nickname, earned thanks to a trick of the light or so the residents who now only numbered 214, claimed.

Ten months ago there were nearly 300 people in the town and what could have been a boom town started to shrink in size and prosperity. They were all taken in by a conman, Jon Fitzroy. His silk tongue convinced most of them to invest in a railroad from St Louis to the Pecos Valley along the old Butterfield

Overland Mail Trail with the Union Pacific Railway. When it didn't materialize after Mr Fitzroy went to St Louis to deposit the money so the work could start straight off, Marshal Jones contacted the Union Pacific.

The railroad company explained, 'We've no plans to build a railroad down there and if we were, we wouldn't consider a stopover in the town because no one would want to step out into Hell.'

Extra hotels, saloons and stores ready to take the railroad passengers with their business and money, stood half built and abandoned to the elements.

A few citizens still prospered: Graham Greenwich who owned the biggest store for several years supplied everyone for miles around; the Last Chance saloon had good trade from the folks who saw no prospects for the future other than to drown their sorrows with the little money they had left; Cutler did well as the barber and surgeon tending wounds from the gunslingers and drifters who came to look for a fight, and Jan Coots, carpenter and undertaker, buried the ones he couldn't patch up.

Marshal Jones reflected that there hadn't been a problem with gunslingers when the Young clan was around. The Bayfield brothers had made sure no townsfolk stepped out of line. It had all changed when Kit Bayfield's boy, Broke, planted all nine of the Young clan in Boot Hill. Russell Bayfield was dead, killed by his pa, and Tyler had disappeared.

The place was getting out of control. The marshal reckoned he was too old for this job.

Things were starting to look bad in Hell but Marshal Jones convinced himself that it couldn't get worse.

It did.

'Marshal Jones, we got a bank robbery happening right now.'

Inside the only bank in Hell, a robbery was taking place. Doady Nixon's gang who travelled the West looking for small towns prosperous enough to have banks to empty, was holding the manager and cashiers at gunpoint.

'You got everyone covered?'

The question came from a man with dark, beady eyes that peeped from under a felt hat and above a neckerchief tied over his lower face.

'Sure have, boss,' another equally well-hidden face answered.

'Got those doors as well?'

A man stood next to the thick wooden doors of the white adobe building. He nodded.

The bank manager, a gun to his head, opened the safe and what was left of the savings of the townsfolk, spilled out. The threat the robbers had made, to shoot him and all the bank clerks, made him co-operate.

'Looks like there isn't much here, Doady.'

'No names, stupid,' Doady muttered.

'Sorry, Mr Nixon.'

Doady Nixon shook his head. Palo Mott looked mystified when it came to understanding anything.

'Townsfolk ain't got much money, Mr . . er.' The bank clerk shut his mouth with a snap before he uttered the bank robber's name. 'I mean they all got took by a conman.'

Doady Nixon strode over to the bank manager.

'You ain't got anything else stashed away?' he asked.

Doady rammed his Colt .45 against the man's chest. The frightened man shook so bad he couldn't even stammer a sentence together, just opened and shut his mouth like a fish in a rain puddle, and an ugly wet patch appeared at the crotch of his pants.

'No, he ain't got anything else. Just fill the bags with what's there.'

The plan to get in, take the money from the safe, and get out before anyone suspected a robbery, continued. There was several thousand dollars and some gold pieces and they had to be satisfied with that. The bags that the manager and clerks tied up as neatly as thanksgiving turkeys were stuffed full of greenbacks and gold, and they were ready to leave. Then, one of the robbers, Roland Lange, got greedy.

When the robbers entered the bank they thought it was empty of customers. They didn't notice the two women waiting to be served. Mrs Molly Payette and

Mrs Lizbeth Tander stayed in the background when they saw the robbers enter the bank, stepped back and kept quiet. However Roland's beady eyes noticed the two hiding behind the desk.

'Well, well, well! What we got here?'

A big, proud-looking woman stepped forward. She held her bag tightly against her chest. 'You ain't taking my money,' Mrs Molly Payette screamed. 'That's about the last few dollars we got in the world after that conman fooled us.'

'It ain't my fault you fell for a four-flusher,' Roland laughed.

He had a reputation in the gang as a hothead but what happened next wasn't too clear. Roland Lange tried to get the woman's purse and Molly Payette, wild as a Kilkenny cat, hit out at the robber. The outcome was a gun went off as they fought. A second later she lay on the floor, blood seeping from a gun wound.

'Get out now,' Doady shouted. 'We'll be lynched.'

Todd Wynham grabbed hold of Roland who stood rooted to the spot like he was going to wake up from a bad dream, and meekly allowed Todd to pull him out the door.

'I didn't mean to shoot . . .' he muttered.

The bank robbers headed off – unhitched their horses as they mounted them. A fog of road dust covered them as they made their getaway down Main Street. Doady, Walter Minke and Andy Pope had the bank money. Todd Wynham slapped the rump of Roland's horse to get it going. Palo Mott cut his spurs deep into his animal's side and followed at top speed.

The marshal heard the sound of the shot from the bank at the same time Deputy Wills ran into the law office.

'Marshal Jones, we got a bank robbery,' he repeated.

The marshal sighed, took his booted feet off the desk and got a rifle from the gun cupboard. He didn't intend to use a fancy six-shooter when this sort of trouble cropped up. 'You arm up with a Winchester, Wills. An' check which end shoots the bullets.'

Wills bristled with indignation. 'I've been practis-ing,' he said. 'I can shoot six outa ten bottles off the log in the yard.'

'OK. Just make sure you fire first and ask questions after.'

The marshal smiled as he went out the door and down the sidewalk to the bank. He looked in no rush to face down a whole gang of desperadoes but when they rode past galloping like the Dickens, he and Wills fired after them. In the bank he found something even a hardened marshal didn't expect to find.

'Get the doc, and Mr Payette,' he said. Marshal Jones shook his head as he examined the bullet holes, which had ricocheted across the room. 'And let get a posse together.

CHAPTER FOUR

As Little Bluestem left Broke after providing him with water she noticed Fighting Bear. She saw him look at his adopted son and believed she saw sorrow in his eyes. It didn't surprise her when, that evening, Black Horse announced that as Broke had survived four days of torture they could give him a chance to stay alive.

'He has earned that right with his courage,' Black Horse said. The words sounded as if they were torn from his lips. Fighting Bear stood nearby and nodded his approval when Broke was cut down. 'We will give him until the sun climbs back over the horizon and then we will come after him.'

A gasp came from Little Bluestem. 'He isn't strong enough to move,' she said.

Black Horse's face contorted with anger. His authority had been questioned by his father and now by the girl who'd caused all this trouble. He frowned.

He hadn't thought it out. Then an evil smile, which didn't reach his eyes, altered his face again. It showed the character of the man he would become. Little Bluestem stepped back, alarmed by the change and aware she had made an enemy of him.

It was then he made his threat to her. He looked at the girl.

'As he is so weak we will allow Little Bluestem to help him, otherwise there will be no sport in it. You can take him away. I'll allow you until the sun goes down again before we give chase. When I catch up with you there will be no question of who you belong to.'

She didn't hesitate and moved to help Broke before Black Horse finished his words. She severed the cruel rawhide that had already cut deep into his flesh and noticed the horse and travois Broke had used to bring a couple of slaughtered deer as an offering for a feast. A blanket tied between the two poles made a comfortable bed for Broke to lie on. She filled a basket strapped at the top of the poles with items that might be useful for their flight. No one helped her but neither did anyone stop her. It was as if she wasn't there. She took advantage of this and hacked tasty morsels of meat from the roasted animal, wrapped it in a piece of soft leather, and filled several water bottles from the nearby stream. Afterwards she hauled the unconscious man on to the travois and mounted the horse, Broke's sturdy

Appaloosa, and rode out. The sun was starting to dip down behind the hills as she left the camp.

She had one night to save Broke from the Comanche.

Little Bluestem heard a moan from the injured man on the travois as it bumped and rattled along the track. She hadn't time to stop. They travelled through the night. She was heading for the mountains. Before the sun set again she had to be far away and tucked safely into a cave. This was what she planned, but she had no idea whether she'd be able to carry it out. The Comanche wouldn't stop hunting for them unless they could get out of their territory. She had had the foresight to take the Henry rifle that Broke carried in the horse's scabbard and his bow and arrows. She also had her own knife, but the weapons wouldn't be enough to keep a whole band of braves away. She'd be able to kill a few if they found her, but without Broke's help, she didn't know how long she could hold out. Little Bluestem tucked away the dark thoughts and got on with the task of increasing the distance between them and their tormentors.

The travois left a deep set of tracks. To disguise them she stopped when she found a couple of leafy branches and fixed them on the travois to disperse the trail. As soon as she could she wanted to move up to the mountain foothills and away from the plains. It would be painful for Broke but unavoidable. At the stop to tie the branches on the travois she infused a little datura and water into tea and fed it to him even though he'd refused it earlier – it would take his pain away and help his body rest and heal. Otherwise Little Bluestem didn't stop. For a few hours she slept sat on the horse's back, but did not dare to stop and rest. As long as the horse moved, she would continue without a stop. Occasionally she walked beside the horse to allow it to rest, but mostly, she forced as much as she could from the animal. It drooled saliva from its mouth and patches of its coat turned white with sweat but it kept going as she gave it water and coaxed it onwards.

The next day before the sun started to set and they still had plenty of light, she got down from the horse and led it along a mountain path. They were both grateful to see a stream as the water bottles were empty, and the horse drank as Little Bluestem rubbed its coat dry. She administered more datura tea to Broke before they continued onwards and upwards. It was almost dark by the time she found a cave. She had to hope it wasn't a bear's hide-out but as the horse gave no signs of distress she went into the mouth of the cave. The horse helped her pull the travois to the back of the shelter and stood motionless as she moved Broke and covered him with a blanket.

Leading the horse back along the trail to the point they'd turned off to the cave, Little Bluestem picked up rocks and stones and weighted the travois again.

The horse waited and watched, as if it sensed what she was doing.

'It's time to say goodbye, my friend.'

The animal neighed and Little Bluestem patted its neck and head and stroked its velvet nose. It had been a good companion to her and Broke. To be without a horse was a death sentence but she had to take into account that the Comanche would use the tracks of the horse to find them. She turned that to her advantage.

'Now, I want you to go as far and as fast as you can. Perhaps we'll meet up again but now its time to save your master.'

A grin came to her face as she imagined Black Horse's fury at finding the riderless steed. Then she slapped its rump with her hand and with a good-natured sounding whinny the horse was off.

There was no moon. A good time to be pitch black and therefore invisible, but she wished she'd had the evening light just a bit longer. Although Black Horse had promised to give them a good start, she couldn't take that for granted and wouldn't risk firing a torch to guide her. She turned and trekked carefully back along the trail and hoped she'd find her way to the cave.

Broke opened his eyes and could see nothing. A moment of panic hit, certain he was blind, but then he got used to the darkness. He could make out a patch of grey, which intensified into a brighter light, in the distance. The last thing he remembered was that someone had cut the rawhide which bound his wrists to the branches of the tree. Lots of words, but nothing made sense. Every movement hurt and although he couldn't see clearly, he could feel the stickiness of his blood, together with the metallic taste in his mouth.

He heard his name. The sound floated towards him and instinctively he reached for a weapon. His Henry rifle was by his side. He picked it up and although his hands hurt to hold the rifle he held it ready to fire in the direction of the sounds. He was naked apart from a blanket he lay on and the one which covered his body. He heard his name again and then the name 'Mary' after it. The name Mary stirred up vague memories. It didn't sound threatening, but he treated it as such and didn't reply. He lay motionless and didn't allow a single movement to betray his presence as the sound came nearer. Broke remained still as if he was part of the rocks on which he lay.

'Broke,' Little Bluestem called. 'It's Mary.'

She surprised herself. She'd discarded that name a long time ago. No one called her Mary. For six years since the age of twelve, she had never heard her own Christian name. And she wasn't sure whether she liked it now.

Yet she was Mary Williamston who had travelled

overland to the west coast. Or had until her parents and brother were killed in an Indian attack on the lone wagon which had been separated from the wagon train because of a broken axle. Her pa, an independent cuss, she recalled, had said they needed no help to fix it and they'd join up with the others later. Sometimes she wondered if the rest of the wagon train had made it over to Oregon but it didn't hold her thoughts for long. She was a no-nonsense type who lived for each day and didn't dwell on the past.

Little Bluestem was the name of a flower on the prairies that the Indian women said reflected the colour of her eyes. She'd received better treatment than other captives because her bright eyes, so different to their own dark brown, fascinated the Comanche women. She took advantage of her youthful appearance, grateful that it made her position with the Comanche easier for her. She'd seen the treatment of other female captives. They were regarded as competitors for the menfolk and the Indian women were worse than men when it came to tormenting a prisoner.

She'd been able to avoid attention from men because they thought her a child: she'd inherited her mother's petite frame and it allowed her to take several years off her age, but the blue eyes that made life easier when the Comanche first captured her, became her downfall. They attracted Black Horse.

Little Bluestem tried to make herself invisible but he'd told her she'd be one of the many wives he could command.

She never stopped looking for a way to escape. She had hoped to get away when the soldiers made the Indians move from their own land. However she'd been hidden from prying eyes and taken to the reservation undetected.

Her mind came back to the present as she finally stumbled across the cave opening. Here she found a pine knot, full of resin, one of a few that she collected as they'd trekked across the plains. The small bits of wood burnt well and brightly and she'd decided to risk the light for a short time. She struck a piece of flint on the rocky wall. A flame lit up the cave and she moved towards him and then knelt at his side.

'Broke. It's Mary. Little Bluestem.' He was awake. There was a note of relief in her voice. 'I had to crawl along in the darkness for a while. I didn't know whether I might disturb a sleeping bear.'

'You have,' he said.

'Yes?'

In answer to her puzzled question he reached out for her. Touched her, as if to make sure she was really there, and not a figment of his imagination. He held her close.

'Little Bluestem.'

Her response was to hold him and they lay

together in the sanctity of the cave. The light splut-
tered and died and they slept. Later she woke and, as
her eyes got used to the dark, Little Bluestem looked
at the sleeping man. His face bore only the pain of
his experiences. A frown on his brow, his lips held
tight even in sleep. His body was badly marked; Black
Horse's knife had nearly peeled the skin from his
chest. It would heal but the scars of the last few days
would remain. She rolled away from his side. She
didn't want to disturb him; his body would heal with
rest. She wrestled with the notion of making a hot
drink, or whether she could make the meat into a
broth, but was concerned a fire, or the smell of
cooking, would lead the Comanche to their hideout.
She had already taken a chance using the light to
guide her to the back of the cave. Broke had to get
fitter before they could move.

Little Bluestem looked through the things she'd
taken from the travois by using her hands rather
than her eyes to guide her search. When she left the
camp she had taken some plants she knew would
help Broke. She'd learnt many things from the
Comanche women in the years she had been with
them. Although the people turned to the medicine
man for chants and charms it was the women who
knew how to look after the braves hurt in battle. It
was their healing plants she would use.

She looked across at the man as she chewed the
leaves carefully making sure not to swallow any or

waste a drop, then she covered his wounds with a poultice which would heal and keep out infections. She washed his wrists and covered those as well. When he stirred in his sleep she paused and then continued the task. The act of caring for Broke gave her strength.

Little Bluestem had always had more than sisterly feelings for him. She had showed him how much she loved him when he'd held her in his arms. He'd helped her settle into the camp and an attachment had developed because of shared adversity. They were prisoners – kidnapped by the Comanche. When Broke left to find his own family he hadn't promised to come back for her, but she knew he would. Now she sought to repay his generosity by healing the wounds that had been inflicted because of her.

She chewed some more plants and when she had a small amount of the masticated leaves, she set them aside and examined the food she'd brought with them. The deer had been cooked well enough to fall away from the bone. One deer had been roasted on a spit for the feast but the second, to eat later, had been wrapped in leaves and buried amongst grass and hot rocks in the ground. It was this meat she'd taken. Little Bluestem was worried that Broke would have trouble swallowing even such tender meat so she wrapped a small amount in the skin she'd carried it in and pulverized it between two rocks.

Broke stirred from his slumbers. When he opened

his eyes again and sat up he found he'd grown used to the lack of light and could make out the companion who sat by his side.

'Feeling better?' she asked. She held out a drink of water and smiled when Broke nodded and sipped at the liquid that he said tasted as sweet as nectar. 'Chew this if you can.'

Little Bluestem gave him the dish of meat mixed together with healing plants. As he slowly ate the paste, he paused and looked at her.

'Did you give me something, apart from water, when I was tied to the tree?'

'Afterwards,' she admitted. 'When I took you from the camp on the travois.' She didn't quite meet his gaze. She had no idea how he'd react. 'I wanted to . . help a friend.'

Broke reached out and held her hand; pulled her close to him again. Her blue eyes stared at the man and her smile, even in the dark cave, was bright.

'Thank you,' he said.

CHAPTER FIVE

'This is a fine spot to hide. Like nobody else would come here, Doady,' Walter Minke said. His gaze took in the jagged rocky skyline and the dark forbidding trees that seemed to hedge them in. He looked around at the vista of mountain ranges interspersed with pine trees. A grey monster streaked with green fissures. He shuddered involuntarily. 'Sorta place that wraps round you like it don't want to let you go.'

Roland Lange stared at Walter. 'It takes some nerve to go into that town of Hell and blast a bank and you come all-overish 'bout staying here?' He shook his head. 'I know where I'd rather be.'

'That town sure made me nervous,' Andy Pope agreed.

'Yeah,' Doady Nixon said. 'I reckon it's sound enough.' The spot seemed perfect when he'd come across it a couple of months ago. He ignored the complaining tone of his friends. Walter always complained and Andy just fell in with what he said. Doady spat out a rabbit bone now picked clean of meat. 'Found it when I was out on a cattle drive, rounding up some dogies.'

The six of them sat round the fire, coffee bubbling in the pot, all congratulating each other about how they'd managed to pull off a good heist. They'd ridden quite a few miles from the bank they'd robbed.

'How much you reckon we got there?' Andy asked.

He stared at the bags of gold and greenbacks, and spittle dribbled from the side of his mouth. His eyes glazed and he looked like he was thinking about what to spend his share on.

'We took about six thousand dollars and a couple more in gold pieces. But there's not enough to make a gal appreciate you an' forget you're a cross-eyed punk,' Doady laughed. You could insult anyone if you'd made them rich, he reckoned. He watched a smile spread over Andy's face. It was like he was anticipating the girls he could get.

Roland Lange busied himself with more practical things. He'd made the fire, put a couple of pans over it, one for coffee the other for beans with the stringy old rabbit Walter had shot chopped into it.

'Why did you dang well shoot that rabbit in the body, Walter?' He spat out a piece of lead. 'You could've shot its head off and killed it just as easily.'

He took his neckerchief, wound it over the palm of his hand, lifted the pot from the fire, and poured a mug of coffee to rinse his mouth.

'Man at the pot,' Todd called. Roland raised his eyebrows but said nothing and filled the other mugs now held outstretched towards him.

Andy blew on his fingers and moaned that the heat from the tin mug made it uncomfortable to hold.

'There's something unsettling about a town with a name like that,' Walter continued as if there had been no break in the earlier conversation. 'I mean the whole place looked weird.'

'Yeah, did you see how it turned red as we were riding away?' Andy asked. 'It was a vision of hell.'

'Well if you're that frightened of things, you'd best take a piss before it gets so dark we have to hold your hand 'case the bogeyman comes after you both!' Roland laughed.

Walter took it personal and wasn't pleased at being made to sound like a fool. His craggy lined face pulled into a grimace, although to those who didn't know him it would be hard to tell that he'd changed his expression.

'Seems to me from the smell of you,' Walter said, 'it was lucky you had brown pants on when you shot that woman.'

Roland dropped his mug of coffee as he sprung to his feet. 'You calling me a yellow-belly?' He held a

41

gun in his hand.

'I'm calling you a fool who killed a woman.' Walter stared as he saw the gun. He didn't have time to clear leather. 'Hell, Roland, I ain't toting a gun.' His gaze went to his gunbelt on the ground. 'At least give me chance to draw.'

Roland put his gun back in its holster and unbuckled his belt.

'OK, Walter, we're equal. Now I want you to take back what you said.'

Walter didn't know how to back down as he continued to argue. 'You put us all in danger being so hot-headed. If it wasn't that the marshal is the same colour as you, yeller—'

Walter didn't finish his words.

Roland was the taller of the two but Walter more than made up for the other's long reach with his squat, strong, heavy body. However he made the mistake of not protecting his bulbous nose, and as Roland's clenched fist smashed into Walter's face, everyone heard the crunch as he hit bone. Blood splashed on to Roland's shirt but he didn't notice. Walter was slow and though he could take punishment, by the time he raised his fist to hit back, Roland had moved. When a punch finally landed it knocked the wind out of Roland. The man staggered and fell to the ground. Walter moved to follow through with a second and third blow that would've finished the fight. Unfortunately his buffalo-like agility made him slow to start and, once he got going, made it difficult to stop. Roland was still on the ground and he stuck his foot out and brought the big man down. His body spun right over and Walter thudded on to his back. Roland took advantage of the fall and climbed on top of him, straddled his chest and grabbed a handful of his hair. He raised Walter's head and punched it, with a clenched fist, from side to side.

Doady, Andy, Todd and Palo watched the spat with detached interest, but when the sixth punch landed, and after Walter had stopped moaning, Doady and Palo pulled Roland off. Walter lay where he fell, his features changed from craggy to something resembling an erupted volcano. His nose skewed and blood poured out his nostrils and it looked as if it needed mending. It wasn't an improvement.

'What did you do that for?' Both Doady and Palo held on to Roland as he was still punching his corner – albeit into the air. 'We managed to escape from Hell without injury and here you are doing to Walter what those townsfolk would've like to have done to us all.'

Eventually Roland stopped his struggles and calmed down but it didn't shut him up.

'You heard him, Doady,' he said. 'I didn't like all the insults he was dishing out. I didn't mean to kill no woman. You saw how she fought like a wild cat and the darn gun went off.'

43

Doady nodded agreement. 'OK, you're even now so let's say no more about it.' He looked at Todd, Palo and Andy. 'We got to stick together. As soon as we've rested up here, we'll share the money and then go our separate ways.'

Andy found a bottle of whiskey, removed Walter's neckerchief and soaked it in alcohol to clean the wounds. It woke him up and he screamed with pain so Andy poured some of the whiskey into the man's mouth to hush him up. He also took a couple of swigs of the fiery liquid as well before, without saying a word, he held on to Walter's nose and clicked the bone back into place. Andy, a small, quick-footed feller, was able to move away before Walter had the chance to lash out at him.

Walter sat up and cursed Andy.

'Stop moaning, the man's trying get that mug back to looking just ugly,' Doady said. He always reckoned Andy could've been a good sawbones if he had given his brain a little use. Doady shrugged his shoulders like it wasn't his concern if people made a mess of their lives. Andy gave Walter the rest of the whiskey so he could nurse his throbbing nose in an alcoholic haze.

Doady forced Roland and Walter to make a truce. 'You can't blame Walter for what he said. There was a lot of truth in it. The bank robbery went seriously wrong because you didn't pistol-whip the woman as soon as she opened her sassy mouth. You give her too much rope and she'd thought she could be a hero.'

Todd added his wisdom about life to the conversation. 'The only time you want a sassy woman is when you're sharing a blanket.'

Although the men shook hands Walter said, 'If I ever see you again after we've shared the money and split up, I'll make it payback time.'

'What's that?' Little Bluestem asked. They both heard a scream of pain coming out of nowhere. They'd made good progress from the cave even though she carried a backpack and Broke was injured. She moved closer to him. 'It sounds like an owl has got its claws into a buck rabbit.'

When they started to investigate, it was Broke who noticed the horses. He reckoned it was a chance to escape the Comanche. Without a horse they were dead. That they'd survived so long was down to Little Bluestem's thorough planning. She'd had the sense to pack the travois with food, medicine, water, weapons and bedding, but now, they had little water to sustain them.

'We'll make our way further along the tree line over there and try to find out what's going on,' Broke said. 'If we can take a horse then we'd make it to the Rocky Mountains before Black Horse catches up with us.'

'We could ask for help,' Little Bluestem suggested.

Broke raised his eyebrows slightly. 'I think that

anyone this far away from a town are hiding themselves. And look at us,' he commented, 'do you think even law-abiding folk would help?'

She followed his gaze. His body wore the marks of his torture. Bloodied, battered and bruised he looked every inch the painted savage. He wore a breechcloth and leggings pushed into moccasins, together with a buckskin jacket. His dark chestnut hair, although no longer plaited, had grown again since he'd had it cut after leaving the Comanche. He shaved his chin in Indian fashion, so he couldn't be mistaken for a trapper. His skin had long ago lost the fair blush denoting his Irish ancestry and he was as dark as an Indian. And who would stay around long enough to notice the ice blue eyes of a paleface?

Little Bluestem wore a buffalo skin shift cleverly beaded for decoration. She'd been taught to sew by her mother and then honed her skills copying the Comanche women. Her hair was oiled and plaited and she too, wore moccasins.

'No,' she agreed. 'No one will help us. We'll have to help ourselves.'

She wanted to go with him to search the area, but he said he didn't want to worry about her as well as any other possible dangers.

'I'll be back before the owl gets another buck rabbit,' he smiled.

She waited while Broke went nearer to find out who was at the camp. He was back as quickly as he'd promised yet in Little Bluestem's mind minutes had stretched into hours.

'There are six horses and a couple of pack animals tied up in trees and six men, one injured, round a campfire,' he said. He frowned. 'I heard them talking about a bank robbery and a shooting. . . .'

'Would it be best to circle round them and avoid them completely?'

'I'll be careful. If I take one horse we're not going to leave them without means of travelling.'

She nodded her head in agreement and they waited for dusk. They'd decided she would make her way past the men camped by the trees, continue up the trail and carry on walking, until Broke, who was going to take a horse, caught up with her together with the stolen animal.

'We'll only be apart for a while,' he assured her.

The pair started on their separate journeys. Broke took the Henry rifle and wore the bow and arrows and Little Bluestem had a Bowie knife in her belt. As she moved forward to avoid the camp, she had the feeling that a thousand eyes were focused on her. The Indians often said it was so, and that the world was full of creatures that never made themselves known. She shivered as she tried to blot out pictures of snakes and wild beasts that might be around. She shook off her misgivings and slipped into the shelter of the trees to avoid being seen. So intent on ignoring these imagined dangers was she that she didn't notice the dried twigs beneath her feet until they cracked and crunched when she stepped on them.

Too late Little Bluestem froze. Her sharp eyes caught a movement in the trees and saw the outline of a man. Whoever it was must have heard the twigs snap and her hand went to the sharp Bowie knife at her waist. The riveted wood handle at the end of the curved six-inch blade fitted snuggly into the palm of her hand. She'd picked up the weapon dropped by a man captured by the Comanche. He'd had no need of it when they'd finished with him.

Her fingers tensed around the handle. She knew how to use it. She'd gutted and skinned enough animals to be very efficient with the weapon and was prepared to use it if she was threatened. What white men did to Indian women was well known and how afterwards, if they were still alive, their own people rejected them. The fear that Broke would rebuff her if this man touched her made her determined not to be captured.

Her lips stuck together, her mouth too dry to swallow, as she waited for something to happen. Nothing moved again. Little Bluestem hoped that whoever was out there thought they'd been mistaken. Perhaps she'd been mistaken. That was it. On that note of relief, her breath came out in a jagged sigh. It was loud enough for her to regret it. As still as a statue she stayed and waited again. Only her eyes scanned the woods around her as she watched for him to search her out.

Unfortunately for her she had been seen and heard. Andy had walked from the camp to find a place to take a piss and was turning back towards the camp-fire when he heard a sound.

His excitement intensified as he stared at the lone woman with her beautiful face and a body that curved in and out in all the right places. Almost as an afterthought he noticed she was an Indian squaw and was immediately on his guard. This wasn't something you came across every day. The Indian women tended to stay close to home and as far as he knew there wasn't an Indian reservation closer than two days' ride away. He knew there was a possibility of a renegade band of savages anywhere in the vicinity and that made him wary. The army was busy herding the Indians into reservations but plenty of young braves were intent on fighting until the bitter end to keep their land. However they didn't usually take squaws with them and as he couldn't see anyone else around he let a whistle of joy escape through his chipped front teeth.

It could be a lucky day for him – they had got a bit of money from the bank robbery and now he'd found a woman to entertain him. She was an Injun of course, but Andy's philosophy was that all cats were black in the dark. This one had frozen with fear and was like a mouse caught in the stare of a snake.

He decided to strike.

CHAPTER SIX

The man walked towards her without trying to hide. It temporarily put her off her guard because she had a notion that he meant her no harm by approaching so openly. Perhaps he hadn't said anything because he didn't want to frighten her, she reasoned.

Then she caught sight of his face.

It leered at her and the thin, slack lips drooled. He didn't seem to notice as he made no attempt to wipe it away and saliva pooled into a dark, damp spot on his shirt. The man made up for a lack of height with a tight muscular frame. His body tensed as if he was about to pounce. Little Bluestem was sure if he got hold of her, she'd stand no chance of escape.

'Hello little lady,' Andy said, his voice husky and low. 'What's your name?'

Little Bluestem didn't answer.

'You lost your tongue?' he said. She remained still and waited for his next move. Irritation flitted across his face. Then he became more relaxed and attempted a smile. 'Or maybe you're shy?' The man moved fast and covered the remaining distance between them in a few seconds. 'Don't be shy with me. Relax and you'll be OK.'

He pinned her in a clinch with one hand and tore at her shift with the other, forcing his mouth down on to her lips. She squirmed against his foul breath.

'Let me go!'

He wasn't listening and pushed her backwards and on to the ground. He straddled above her as he took off his belt and started to unbutton his pants. Little Bluestem tried to use the chance to escape but she hadn't moved a couple of inches before he caught hold of her, bent over and pushed up her skirt. She fought as hard as she could but he was stronger and he pinned her down with his body. It didn't stop her wriggling to make it as difficult as possible for him.

'You little bitch. Keep still.'

One hand bunched into a fist. A mistake. She was able to free her hand.

The curved blade of the Bowie sliced him from his stomach to his chest, and was out again before he had time to squeal. A surprised look, eyebrow arched and mouth opening to form a question, never to be asked, washed over his face before he fell on to her, writhing in his death throes. Little Bluestem pushed him from her. She rolled away in revulsion, splashed by his blood and, horrified by the act of murder, she emptied her stomach of its paltry contents.

Broke was at her side. He put his arm around the wretched girl.

'I've just killed a man. He attacked me.'

'You're all right?' She nodded. 'Well done,' he said.

She looked at him in disbelief.

'It had to be,' he said. He took in her dishevelled appearance. 'What do you think would've happened if he'd overpowered you?'

She didn't answer. She shuddered. She knew.

'Sometimes you have to do what you wouldn't normally do.'

Little Bluestem nodded. 'I wouldn't have wanted an experience with him to be my first time,' she said. Then she looked around. 'Why are you here? Where's the horse?'

'Change of plan,' he explained. 'When I made my way across, I saw them fighting and this time I stopped to watch and listen. There was a shooting at the bank robbery. I think they killed a woman in Hell.'

'What's that to you? You always told me how you hated the folks who deserted you.'

'A few people were good to me, like Crosland Page of the Lazy Z Ranch and his daughter, Lizbeth. I want to find out for certain if she's all right. It could've been her, 'cause she's the only one I know crazy enough to challenge a mean man.' He looked at the body on the ground. 'Except you.'

Little Bluestem closed her eyes. Then she opened them and looked at Broke. 'I've no regrets.'

'That's good.'

'But, Broke,' she said, 'even if they have shot your friend Lizbeth, you can't bring her back.'

'I can give the family the satisfaction of retribution. They helped me. I ought to show my regards to them.'

'What are we going to do now?' Little Bluestem didn't argue with him. She knew he was a man of honour. He'd proved that with his return to the Comanche camp for her.

'Thanks to you I've got my Henry rifle. What else do we have?'

'I brought your handgun and we have the bow.'

'Can you use the Colt if we need to fight it out?' Broke asked.

She held up the bloody knife. 'Better than a gun,' she said.

Broke nodded. 'Yes, I want to take them back alive, to hang. Guns only as a last resort.' He looked at the dead body. 'I'll use arrows to wound them. They won't be expecting an attack. Stay back. If one of them breaks loose, feel free to take him down. And, Little Bluestem. . . .'

'Yes?'

'Try not to kill them all with that knife.'

He smiled down at her then kissed her forehead.

*

'Where's Andy got to?' Doady asked.

'Gone to look at the stars or summat,' Roland said. 'An' he's probably got to thinking about all those gals he's gonna meet and have to pay for.'

'He ought to keep his mind off gals out here. Drive him crazier than a run-over raccoon,' Doady said.

He poured another cup of coffee, grimaced and said the stuff was strong enough to dissolve his stomach, but knocked it back anyway. He reflected back to his years as a cowboy riding the trail, out in all weathers and eating all sorts of victuals from the chuck wagon, sleeping on the ground, swallowing dust and flies following the cattle. Bank robberies were a faster, surer way of getting rich. Now, thanks to Roland, the shadow of the gallows was cast over them all. It might have been Roland who pulled the trigger but folks didn't make fine distinctions like that. They'd all swing if they were caught. This stopping-off place was now just that, they needed to move on tomorrow.

Walter's moans brought Doady back to the present. The man had been in a stupor since Roland hit him. Doady told the others he'd leave Walter here if he weren't fit to travel tomorrow. There were no volunteers to stay with the injured man. Anyway, Doady reckoned he'd be fit come morning 'cause he was probably full of the whiskey Andy had used to wipe his wounds and pour down his throat for the pain.

'You think he'll be all right?' Roland asked.

'Add him to the notches on your belt if he isn't,' Doady replied.

Roland's displeasure showed in his scowl but no one went against Doady. 'I ain't kilt that many,' he said. 'Some people just get in the way.' Doady shook his head. Roland had a large space in his head that common sense ought to have filled. He reckoned brains weren't something Roland had managed to get hold of when he was created.

Roland went on to blame everyone, from his ma and no-good pa, to his great-great-grandpappy, for his misfortunes in life, when Doady suddenly sensed that they had company. The hair on the back of his neck stood up.

'Hush,' he whispered. Palo's hand went to his gun. Todd looked round.

Doady felt rather than heard a whoosh sound and he saw Roland fall sideways clutching his shoulder. 'What the. . . ?' His hand went to his gun. The second whoosh saw his hand pinned to the leather holster by his shirt cuff. The other two, Todd and Palo didn't move.

Broke used the arrows to disable the two nearest the injured man, but now he moved forward, Henry rifle pointed at all of them.

'Stay where you are,' he said. 'Drop your guns on the ground where I can see them. One movement that I don't like and I'll fire this rifle. If you not sure whether I can fire all the sixteen bullets before you kill me, go ahead and see.'

No one offered any arguments to a man who carried both a Henry rifle and a bow as weapons. Doady lifted his hand, that wasn't restrained by the arrow, to show he had no other weapon. He wanted to make it clear that he didn't want to provoke the Indian. Roland, his brainpower not increased by the arrow in his shoulder, shouted and cussed and told the 'Injun' he'd kill him once he got the arrow out. Broke still watched the other three but stepped forward and reached down and pulled the arrow. The man flinched with the pain as the barbs came out.

'You feel ready to fight now?' Broke asked. Roland's conversation suddenly dried up. He didn't respond to the challenge. 'I thought not.'

'What do you want, Injun?' Doady pleaded. 'I got some firewater and a couple of guns you can have.'

'I heard you talk about a bank robbery and a shooting,' Broke answered. 'I want you to tell me all about it.'

Doady shook his head. 'I don't know anything about a bank robbery.'

The bluff didn't work. Broke swiftly replaced his Henry rifle in its scabbard, securely over his shoulder, and reached for his bow and arrows. 'I can refresh your memory. You'll tell me the truth with a few more arrows in you. I can keep you alive for a long time. You'll be begging for that firewater to quell the pain if you don't answer my questions.' Broke placed the arrow in his bow and aimed it towards the man. 'So what's it to be?'

Doady Nixon seemed to weigh up the situation and quickly came to the conclusion that all the odds were against him. Todd however saw a chance when he saw Broke replace his Henry rifle in its scabbard. He dived to the ground after his gun. He was quick. Not fast enough against yet another gun. A blast from a Winchester double action rifle hurled the gun across the ground – Todd's hand was still holding it.

Todd Wynham rolled and screamed with agony.

'You,' the newcomer said to Palo Mott, one of the only robbers on his feet and uninjured, 'stop the bleeding. I want to take that feller to see the hangman.'

Broke looked at the man and smiled.

'Nice timing,' he said.

'Always knew you'd be at the centre of any trouble,' Gil Tander said.

'And what are you doing here, my friend?'

'After these *amigos*. They pulled off a bank robbery in Hell,' Tander explained. 'Upset the boss on several counts. He had some money deposited at the bank. That doesn't sit too well with Crosland Page. And he doesn't want the bank advertising itself as an easy target.'

'So how much has he lost?'

'Nothing, they were so dumb they didn't notice the bag of money counted out ready for Lizbeth. I was in the store down the street and just gonna pull the wagon over to the bank.'

'You hear that, Palo? You great fool – we could've got more!'

'Wouldn't have done you much good,' Broke observed. 'You'd still be going back to Hell with the money.'

Little Bluestem joined Broke at the camp-fire and he introduced Gil Tander to her. 'He's the foreman at the Lazy Z. He helped me out when I left the Comanche.'

'We'll help you take these back to Hell,' Broke said.

'Is it far to Hell? Will the Comanche follow us there?'

'What's this about the Comanche?' Tander asked.

' 'Fraid I upset them when I went back to get Little Bluestem. We have to get to the Rocky Mountains before they catch us.'

Doady eyes widened as he scanned the landscape. 'You mean there are more savages around here?'

'I don't think they are far away. Let's hope they don't find us,' Broke said. 'You might not think it's a good idea to come back with us but sure beats staying here and have the Comanche take you to their idea of hell.'

Doady offered Broke and Gil Tandy a share of the money they'd stolen if they'd let him go. For an answer to that suggestion, Broke shot an arrow at Doady and the man squirmed in fear. He wasn't hurt. Broke grinned as he retrieved the arrow from between Doady's legs.

'I'm taking you back to answer for your crimes,' Gil Tander said.

They secured Doady with a lariat from his own horse, to Roland. The pair sat back-to-back, diamond hitched together. They did the same to Palo Mott and Walter. The bloodied and bleeding Todd Wynham sat with a tourniquet around his arm and wasn't about to move anywhere. Andy Pope was dead as a tin of corned beef but they decided to take him in as well. They didn't want the chore of burying him and reckoned no one would be standing in line to offer a prayer for his soul. As Broke and Tander dragged the body to lie across the horse, Broke noticed bloodstains the foreman's shirt.

'One of them caught me in the shoulder a while back,' he said. Gil looked older than Broke remembered but then he figured he'd been wounded.

'I'll take the bank robbers to town, Gil,' Broke said. 'You ride with us part the way and then go to the Lazy Z.'

Gil nodded. 'I'll take you up on that,' he said.

'Join us for some food, Mr Tander,' Little

Bluestem said. 'And I have something to go over that wound to keep it clean.'

In the short time it took for Broke and Gil Tander to secure the outlaws, Little Bluestem had killed several rabbits, which were busily cooking in a large stewpot. A pot of coffee bubbled ready. She'd used the outlaw's supplies to make the brew.

'This sure beats that pulped up mush you fed me back in the cave,' Broke said. He wiped the meat juices that dripped down his chin with the back of his hand.

'That was to heal your body,' Little Bluestem smiled. She took a bite of the tender flesh. 'This is good for the soul.'

CHAPTER SEVEN

Little Bluestem knew Broke to be a man of few words. When they'd been together in the Comanche band they'd lived in the present not the past. The ride to Hell allowed her a further glimpse of his former life. She listened as he chatted to Tander.

'Mister Page recovered from all the trouble he suffered?' Broke asked.

'Place is bigger than ever. We rent land off the Comanche as you suggested and been able to increase our stock of longhorns. Ain't all plain sailing; those young braves are restless on the reservations, and make things difficult. Sometimes I reckon we got the wrong pig by the tail.'

Broke nodded in agreement but said nothing.

'An' Miss Lizbeth done me the honour of becoming Mrs Tander,' Gill added.

'Congratulations,' Broke said.

As they rode on with the outlaws, Broke pointed

towards a spread of land with a large ranch house on it. 'The land over there belongs to the Three Bay Ranch. It was just a homestead when the Comanche kidnapped me as a boy. Over the way through Dead Man's Gulch, is the Lazy Z Ranch.' He turned towards Gil Tander. 'This is where you turn off. Give my regards to everyone.'

Tander said Crosland Page would be happy with the news about the bank robbers. He invited Broke to call in when he was passing the ranch.

Broke went quiet as they made their way towards the town and Little Bluestem filled the silence with her own story.

'We were travelling to Oregon. I recall Ma wanted to take the railroad, but Pa insisted we had to save money and anyhow he didn't trust those iron monsters, so we joined up with a small wagon train. It was all right until our wagon got damaged going over some rutted tracks.' She paused for a moment. 'Well you know the rest. I was tiny, they reckoned I was younger than I was, and I was given to a Comanche squaw as a present.'

Broke took a long look at his travelling companion. She was petite and at a glance, a child. But when they'd nestled together for comfort and he'd held her in his arms in the cave, he'd noticed her body had ample curves shrouded by the tunic she always wore.

'How old are you?' he asked.

'Eighteen years,' she said.

He smiled, like she'd given him some good news.

Broke had told Little Bluestem he wasn't welcome in Hell.

When they rode into town they certainly attracted attention. Little Bluestem sat behind Broke holding on to him for support and looked about her. Behind them Doady and Roland, the injured Walter and Todd Wynham, plus Palo Mott looked around as well. It hadn't been so long since they'd left and they didn't look happy to be back. The dead eyes of Andy, his body sliced open by the Bowie knife, saw no one.

'This town don't look too bad, Broke,' Little Bluestem commented.

'Some people reckon the town is cursed.'

Little Bluestem shuffled up closer to Broke in the saddle like she was scared.

A sound of aggression was in the ugly hum of voices that greeted their arrival. Broke knew he was near unrecognizable to most of the townsfolk. He'd left Hell, and the Lazy Z Ranch, a year ago. Since then he'd lived in the wilderness, been tortured and now found himself on the run from the Comanche. He knew the picture he presented and could understand the reaction.

'Are those the outlaws who robbed the bank? What are the Injuns doing with them?'

'We've had enough trouble here. We don't want anymore.'

'Looks like you ain't welcome here,' Doady Nixon laughed.

'Not surprised by dat.' Walter's nasal voice squeaked in their ears.

Broke shifted slightly in the saddle, 'You keep it quiet back there,' he snarled. He lifted his Henry rifle and shook it at them to underline his threat.

Broke had stirred up a lot of bad memories when he'd first returned and although he had helped the marshal to clean up the town, he was aware of the collective sigh of relief when he had left. They ignored everyone and travelled up Main Street until they reached the law office.

The marshal stared, blinked and then recognized Broke.

'What you doing back here, Mitch Bayfield? Can't you stay away?' Marshal Jones asked. He didn't call him by his Comanche name. 'And what's that you're dragging behind you?'

'Looks like I'm doing your job again, Marshal.' Broke's reply sounded snappish. 'Caught up with these outlaws when I was being chased by the Comanche. Heard them say they robbed the bank and killed a woman. I hear Miss Lizbeth was at the bank as well.'

'The Comanche are after you?' Marshal Jones hadn't seemed to register the other things Broke told

64

him. He looked out from Hell, sandwiched between the Pecos River and the Rocky Mountains, as if seeking the dark shadows of the Indians. 'Bad luck surrounds you. Caused a deal of problems last time.'

Broke didn't contradict him. He had a notion that Marshal Jones would never thank him for getting rid of the Young clan, or stopping his stepbrothers, Tyler and Russell, from terrorizing the town. Then the marshal added, almost as an afterthought, 'Lizbeth is doing just fine. It was poor Mrs Payette, the laundry woman, who got the short straw.' He stared at Broke. 'You don't aim to cause that family grief by going there again, do you?'

Broke didn't mention Gil Tander's invitation to visit and there was no reason for him to think Broke would be unwelcome at the Lazy Z Ranch, but Marshal Jones's manner indicated that he didn't want him around. Broke was a thorn in his side, and a constant reminder that the town of Hell had given up on a boy kidnapped by the Comanche and just carried on with their own lives as if nothing had happened.

'No, I ain't hanging around. The two of us will be gone before nightfall. We'll be leaving Hell soon as we dropped these with you.' He pointed to the outlaws. 'One's dead, another two are ready to step off into the next world unless Doc gets to look them over. That feller says he can't breathe none too well but it don't stop him talking any. And, of course, I don't want to deprive you of the pleasure of hanging him. The other lost his hand when he dropped his gun. The other two are alive and well, at the moment.'

'Where's the money they stole from the bank?'

Marshal Jones walked along the row of horses to inspect the captives.

'In the saddle-bags,' Broke said.

'Suppose you'll be expecting the big reward for these fellers?'

'I'll take two fresh horses, a packhorse, and get some supplies from the general store and leave the bill with you. Keep the rest.'

Little Bluestem slipped down from the horse and Broke dismounted afterwards. The marshal stared with a look of disbelief on his face. It appeared he hadn't noticed the girl or heard Broke say 'the two of us'.

'Is this why the Comanche are after you? You stole one of their damn squaws?'

Broke took two steps to get face to face with the marshal. 'This *damn squaw* is a white girl and she's with me.'

'OK, OK, you keep calm, boy. I don't mean anything. Thought she was an Injun.'

Broke knew that nothing had changed in Hell. No one liked the Indians. He'd have to keep Little Bluestem close in case anyone else mistook her for one. They made their way across the street as Marshal

Jones and his deputy, Don Wills, ordered the outlaws to dismount and then locked them in jail, but Broke couldn't miss the furious look Deputy Wills gave him together with the indignation that had him foaming at the mouth. When Maisy Martin had let Broke out of jail, Wills had not been too popular with the marshal for a while.

'I'll make sure these outlaws don't escape, Marshal Jones. No one's gonna call me a beefhead again, an' I can't afford to lose more pay.'

Broke pushed open the door of Graham Greenwich's General Store with its familiar smells wafting about the place: coffee, leather boots, pickled fish, dried meat, and cotton fabric.

This time, a crowd of men, sitting around with their feet up on the stove, swaddled in tobacco and flatulence, and drinking coffee, hadn't heard about Broke's return to Hell and were still there. They all stared in silence at the couple.

Graham Greenwich rushed over from behind the counter to greet them. 'I've always made you welcome, Mitch, er, Broke,' Greenwich said, 'but I can't upset my customers by having a squaw in here, touching things, an' all. It ain't right.'

'If I reflect rightly, Mr Greenwich, you'd leave the place empty rather than have anything to do with me when I came to town last time. This girl is with me. She'll need to buy woman's stuff so you get your wife to serve her what she wants.'

Broke was a big man. He'd grown in strength and courage in his time with the Comanche and his year on the mountains. On his last visit to Hell he'd proved his ability with knife and gun. Greenwich's face pulled into a frown like he needed to mull these things over.

'I'll shut the shop so you can have some privacy,' he said. He looked towards the stove. 'I'll send those old folks out as well.'

Broke put a hand on Greenwich's arm to stop him. 'I don't want it spread over town that we're here. Give them some fresh coffee and tobacco. Put it on the bill.'

'You got no credit here,' the storekeeper said.

'The marshal is paying. I'll wait here while you check it out.'

'No need.' Greenwich looked flustered. His gambit at being able to refuse credit hadn't worked. 'I'll have to see whether Mrs Greenwich is available,' he said.

Graham Greenwich disappeared behind a curtain to a back room. Broke and Little Bluestem looked at each other as they heard muffled arguments. After a short while a woman came out, red faced and snorting like a buffalo. She went over to Little Bluestem.

'My husband says I've got to serve you. We don't stock any Injun clothes. Most of our ladies buy a bolt of material and run up a dress or take it to a dressmaker.' She paused for breath. 'Not that you'll be staying that long.' It wasn't a question. 'But I have a reserve of clothes that might suit. Point to what you want, I'll get it and parcel it up, but if you find it don't fit when you try it on, don't bring it back.'

CHAPTER EIGHT

Little Bluestem had stood quietly next to Broke during the exchange with the storekeeper and now listened to the woman's harsh words. She smiled at her. 'Thank you, ma'am,' she said. 'I only need some plain travelling clothes.'

The reply brought the woman to a stop. She'd pushed past Little Bluestem and was on her way to the shelves. She turned round to face her and without a word stepped up close. She licked her finger and pressed it down on the girl's cheek. Under the layers of trail dust her skin looked paler than she'd expected. The woman peered into the bright blue eyes.

'You ain't no Injun squaw,' she said. 'Mister Greenwich, you come over here. We got a white girl. What's he doing with a white girl?'

She glared at Broke. Her arms went round Little

Bluestem's shoulders and she gripped her like a long lost daughter. Little Bluestem squirmed uncomfortably.

'I told you, it's Mitch Bayfield, not an Injun,' Mr Greenwich said. 'He's the same as us.'

Mrs Greenwich looked at Broke.

'That fact does not reassure me, Mr Greenwich. Not one little bit. However, if he is the same as us, he'll not object to this girl having a bath to wash the stink of Injun out of her.'

Broke shrugged his shoulders.

'You decide what to do, Little Bluestem. I'm gonna get some clothes and head over to the bath house behind Cutler's barber shop.'

'Little Bluestem? What sort of name is that? You got a proper name?' Mrs Greenwich interrupted rudely.

'It's my Comanche name,' Little Bluestem said. 'I was known as Mary Williamston.'

'Well Mary it is,' Mrs Greenwich said. She held on to Little Bluestem's arm and dragged her towards the stairs leading to the second floor.

She was shown into a sparsely furnished room, with a bed, a chair and a chest of drawers, and told to undress while Mrs Greenwich filled a tin tub with hot water. Used to diving into a river or dabbling her feet into a stream to wash, Little Bluestem didn't protest about this luxury.

As she relaxed in the tub she lay back and allowed

Mrs Greenwich to wash her hair. She enjoyed her comments about its thick texture, length and colour but was uncomfortable with the questions the woman asked.

'How come you were with those savages?' Her curiosity was insatiable and she wouldn't relent until Little Bluestem, or Mary, as the woman insisted on calling her, narrated the story of her folk's death at the hands of the Indians when they were left behind on the wagon train.

'After I saw both Pa, Ma and my older brother killed,' she said, 'The Indians took me. I lived with them for many years before Broke rescued me.'

'You weren't taken as a . . .' Mrs Greenwich hesitated. Little Bluestem noticed the embarrassment on the woman's face but waited for her to continue. 'I mean y-you weren't one of those savages, well I mean you weren't one of their wives?'

Little Bluestem shielded the water from her eyes as a jug of warm water was tipped over her head to rinse the soap from her hair. Mrs Greenwich offered her a towel.

'No. They thought I was younger than I am. The Comanche admire children and look after them whatever their race.'

She stared at the woman who'd only been friendly towards her because she was white. However Mrs Greenwich seemed to miss the irony of her comments and continued to tell tales of the terrible things that had befallen other women unlucky enough to fall foul of the Indians.

'Well, I suppose it don't matter none what happened to you. No respectable man will marry you after you being a Comanche squaw for all those years. It's a blessing that Mitch Bayfield likes you.'

Little Bluestem took the towel from Mrs Greenwich's hands with more force than was considered polite. The woman didn't seem to notice.

'I've put out clothes for you to wear.' She picked up the tunic Little Bluestem had taken off and held it between finger and thumb as if it was a wild animal about to bite. 'I'll get rid of these.'

Little Bluestem had no time to protest as the woman left the room and took the tunic away before she was able to ask her to save it.

Almost reluctantly she left the tub of warm soapy water, dried her body on the soft towel, then dressed in the clothes Mrs Greenwich considered more acceptable. She didn't feel comfortable in Mrs Greenwich's idea of 'the right clothes to wear'. The dress with its lace-trimmed collar scratched her neck and she almost tripped over its floor length skirt as she moved carefully down the steps to the store where Broke waited for her. He stared at the picture she presented but passed no comment.

'I think I'd prefer a riding outfit,' Little Bluestem said. She lifted a foot decked in a tiny shoe. 'I need sturdier boots. Or maybe I'll have my moccasins back.'

Mrs Greenwich pursed her lips. 'Your burnt complexion, although lighter than an Injun's, don't suit nice white ladies clothes,' she agreed. She handed Little Bluestem a blue chambray cotton shirt, a long brown wool jacket, a matching divided skirt plus a pair of black boots. 'Perhaps you ought to stay out of the sun and wind in future.'

She thought she saw Broke smile, but his eyes were focused on studying hats so she merely thanked the woman and went to change her clothes. When she returned Broke handed her a dark brown hat with a large brim. 'Keep the weather from hurting your skin,' he said.

'That's a man's hat,' Mrs Greenwich said. 'I'll find you a bonnet.'

Little Bluestem pushed the hat firmly on to her head. 'This'll suit well enough,' she said.

Broke had found a bowler hat to replace the one lost at the Comanche camp. 'I think a brave took a shine to my old hat,' he said. 'I definitely saw someone dancing round the fire with it on their head.' The new one looked better because he'd had a fight with a grizzly bear and other bowler hat bore claw marks across the crown. He'd found a pair of pants to replace the leggings, although he kept the breechcloth underneath, and wore a buckskin jacket over a white shirt. He chose plain all-weather boots fashioned from black leather and a sturdy belt to

74

hold his Colt gun, for which he'd helped himself to plenty of ammunition.

While Little Bluestem had the storekeeper make up a good parcel of supplies, Broke chose a pack horse from the livery stables to carry them all. He reckoned the marshal wouldn't be too put out by the bill they'd send – the reward for the thieves, dead or alive, would probably more than cover the expenses. Broke didn't care about counting dollars or cents and he reckoned Marshal Jones would profit from it.

They had dinner before they left. Lou Neal, who introduced herself as a friend of Maisy Martin, had met them in Graham Greenwich's General Store whilst buying supplies. Lou had ignored Greenwich's protestation that he was not open for business and entered the store. She recognized Broke from Maisy's description and invited him, and Little Bluestem, to eat at her diner. 'It's only a small place, Lou's Diner, next to the Last Chance Saloon, but I recommend the food.'

Broke and Little Bluestem found the diner homely. It boasted about a dozen tables all covered in red gingham cloths. Lou turned the sign to 'closed' and locked the door when they stepped in. 'Unlike Greenwich Stores, when I say no one else can enter, I mean it,' Lou said. 'And you can enjoy a good supper here.' Lou showed them to a table away from the door and window. 'Nice and private and much better than supping elsewhere, 'cause I know some folks would sit and stare. I suppose they're all curious as to why you're here.' Broke nodded in agreement. Lou told them what was on the menu. She continued to chatter as she took the order. 'And I'm so pleased you got Maisy to leave. I don't know what you did but it worked.'

Broke smiled but didn't give any information.

'I hear you brought those bank robbers in? Mrs Payette's husband will be standing at the foot of the gallows to see justice done. An' thank goodness that bullet didn't do any major damage to Miss Lizbeth, or should I say, Mrs Tander.'

Broke's smile faded.

'She's hurt?' he asked. 'Gil never mentioned anything about it.'

'A tiny graze on her arm, where the bullet clipped her, that's all. The bullet went straight through dear Mrs Payette and bounced off the wall to catch Lizbeth. It knocked her off her feet.'

His blue eyes darkened with fury.

Lou had a notion she'd said enough. She left them and went to get the food they wanted.

'I should go to that jail and kill them,' he said.

'You've done what you should. Let the marshal deal with them.'

'If I'd known – if Gil had told me. . . .'

'You'd be the one languishing in jail,' Little Bluestem said.

Lou interrupted further conversation as she he placed a bowl of chicken and dumplings and a basket of hot biscuits and brought a couple of beers to the table before she left them to eat. 'I hope you'll enjoy this. It's the best in town, so I'm told. You just holler if you want anything else.'

Little Bluestem was glad of the distraction of food and thanked Lou for it. She didn't want Broke to do anything that would see him swinging from the end of a rope.

'Thanks for the hospitality. We sure do appreciate it,' she said.

They were hungry, because apart from roast rabbit, the previous evening, they hadn't had much in the way of food. They didn't speak as they ate the chicken and mopped up the gravy with the biscuits.

'You looked good in that dress,' Broke said when they were finished. Little Bluestem grimaced.

'What? All that lace, and a hem so long I'd fall flat on my face as I waltzed out the door?'

'Well, a few alterations might be needed,' he admitted.

'A few! Quicker to make a whole new dress.'

'Look, what I'm saying is that it ain't too late to change your mind about travelling with me. You could get the coach and ride out of here. The Comanche would never recognize you all fancied up.' His face was serious. 'Then you'd be safe.'

'Broke, thank you for your concern,' she said. 'But where do you suggest I go and what do I do when I get there? I haven't lived the life of a white woman for a long time. Like Mrs Greenwich was kind enough to tell me, I wouldn't fit in. And definitely no man would want me. But I could take my chances out there alone. Especially if you want to go visit Miss Lizbeth.' She looked towards the window and across at the distant foothills of the Rocky Mountains. 'I can live, same as always, like an Indian. They taught me how to look after myself.' As she spoke she became more annoyed. 'So, Broke, don't worry about me. I won't slow you down.'

Broke saw her as if for the first time. She looked beautiful. Her hair fell around her face in graceful curls. She'd tied it back loosely but it highlighted her features like a golden frame. He became conscious of staring at her and gave her a big grin to hide his awkwardness.

'You will probably find a young man and have a home, a family . . . and as far as Miss Lizbeth is concerned, she's Mrs Gil Tander and it was never going to be anything else.'

Little Bluestem flushed with embarrassment. 'You must think I'm full of balderdash,' she said.

'No, you're a real nice girl. I wanted to give you the chance to make yourself a better life and it wouldn't be fair to expect you to hang around 'til I decide what I want to do,' he explained.

'I'm not sure of the future either, so, if you don't mind, I'll take my chances with you.'

CHAPTER NINE

Second Lieutenant Rodger Halcomb of the 3rd US Cavalry watched the comings and goings in Main Street, with intense curiosity. Perched on a chair on the boardwalk outside the hotel, next to the law office and across from Graham Greenwich's General store, he focused on the two 'Indians'.

The lieutenant and his troop of soldiers from Fort Concho were on a march to join Colonel Ranald Slidell Mackenzie in the Palo Duro Canyon. Colonel Mackenzie's scouts had discovered the Indians were using the canyon to store horses and supplies to enable them to continue their fight against the white settlers. He'd sent for as many soldiers as he could muster for an attack to decimate them.

He continued to observe the man and the young woman as they stepped out of the store wearing conventional clothes. He'd seen them when they first arrived in town about two hours before and they'd been completely different. Indians, that's how he'd have described them. The man was ruggedly handsome but the woman was something else. Halcomb wasn't happy. The whole thing didn't sit right. He watched them for a while as they went in the direction of the livery stables, and then he got off the comfortable chair on the hotel boardwalk to march half-a-dozen paces to the law office.

Marshal Jones frowned as the soldier stepped into his office. He remained seated. Best way to hear bad news, he'd always said. Over the years folks said the marshal had developed the knack of smelling trouble. It didn't mean of course that he went after it. The nearer he got to retirement the further away he moved away from the smell of it.

'I'm Second Lieutenant Rodger Halcomb, sir.'

He saluted and Marshal Jones waved his hand.

'Sit down, Mr Halcomb,' he said.

'Lieutenant Halcomb, I'll stand, thank you.'

'Sorry, I meant Sergeant Halcomb. Is this official business you're on?'

'I am on a top secret mission, Marshal, which doesn't come under your jurisdiction,' the soldier replied. Marshal Jones sighed with relief. 'However, I need to report something that disturbs me in this town, and ought to concern you.'

Only the marshal's eyebrows moved, they went upwards in the vicinity of his disappearing hairline, his feet remained on his desktop. 'Now what would worry me about Hell?' The marshal's moustache didn't hide a sardonic smile. 'Lived in Hell all my life and I'll probably end up in hell when I die.'

The Lieutenant ignored the joke. 'I saw two Indians ride into town this morning. They brought several outlaws in tow.'

This time the marshal put his feet to the floor and sat up it his chair. 'This top secret stuff of yours doesn't keep you very busy,' he said.

'My men and I are here for a stopover to rest the horses. And whatever the job in hand, I'm trained to notice everything.'

The marshal sighed again before he explained about the two people the soldier was concerned about.

'They are both white. Broke was born Mitch Bayfield and the girl, Mary Williamston, was travelling to Oregon many years ago when she was kidnapped. There's not a drop of Indian blood in their veins. They aren't a problem, Sergeant Halcomb. Leastways, not yours.'

The soldier didn't agree. 'If she's white like you say, she must have folks and well, she ought to be with them. Not roaming the hills with savages.'

Marshal Jones had a different view. He'd be happy when there was a good deal of distance between them and the town; especially as their presence could find the place overrun with renegade

Comanche braves.

'Mrs Greenwich, who left here not five minutes ago, told me all about the girl. She'd been travelling, as I told you, to Oregon with her family when their wagon was attacked. Seems the fool father had risked coming overland when the Indians were on the warpath with settlers. She was the only survivor but taken by the Indians. Anyway that's how it is – she's got no one.'

'A good white family would help her. Get her settled with the right man.'

'Got yourself in mind, Sergeant Halcomb?'

'Second Lieutenant Halcomb if you please, and no, of course not.' He sounded offended. 'I wouldn't want a girl who'd lived with Indians and is probably a savage herself.'

'Exactly, I imagine it's the thought of a fair number of men. Life is tough without having to tame a woman as well.'

Marshal Jones put his feet on his desk and leaned back in his chair again. He reached down for a bottle of 'medicine' from the drawer. As far as he was concerned, the conversation was over, and he ignored the Lieutenant. Halcomb watched the marshal's practiced actions as he poured the glass of whiskey. The routine, so smooth and easy, indicated that the drawer was used frequently. The marshal let the liquid slide down his throat, shook his head and closed his eyes as if the problem might disappear. It did eventually, as far as the marshal was concerned, when Second Lieutenant Rodger Halcomb left his office.

The soldier strutted across the street to the general store, to ask Mrs Greenwich a few questions.

He was annoyed by Marshal Jones's attitude that it was easier to leave things well alone. There was obviously a damsel in distress, and he, Second Lieutenant Rodger Halcomb, wouldn't rest until he'd rescued her. He considered a few days' detour, if necessary, to rescue a white woman, to be acceptable.

Mrs Greenwich was happy to answer his questions. She told her husband that she'd had more excitement today than she'd had for a long time. She didn't notice folks in the store laugh when Mr Greenwich looked offended by the remark.

The more the lieutenant found out about the girl, the more he was determined to save her from her fate. True, he admitted to Mrs Greenwich, she'd been set free from the Comanche but she was with an uncivilized brute.

Several of the lieutenant's men stood at the bar of the Last Chance Saloon and watched their commanding officer stride away from the lawman's office and march towards the general store. Although Halcomb's pace was brisk he still had time to pull at the cuffs of his smart white gloves and brush a speck of dust from his dark blue pants, which were neatly tucked into polished leather boots.

His men pantomimed his actions. A lot of com-missioned officers, like the enlisted soldiers, wore sky-blue pants, but men like their commanding officer shied away from this practice. He'd said, in their hearing, that he had no wish to be mistaken for a common soldier.

The antics and laughter stopped when Halcomb entered the general store and enlisted soldier, Sergeant Bert Stackhouse, ordered another round of beers from the barkeep.

'Looks as if the lieutenant has swallowed a horn toad backwards,' he said. 'Not content with his orders to march us all to Palo Duro Canyon, I reckon he's found us something else to do 'cause he's grittin' his teeth like he could bite the sights off a sixgun.'

'Yo' sure he ain't grittin' his teeth 'case that horn toad comes back up to bite him?' Syd Turnkey laughed.

Unlike Stackhouse, Turnkey sipped at his beer. The sergeant had over twenty years on the boy when it came to drinking. He downed his beer in one go and ordered another before the mug hit the counter. Stackhouse had a drinker's nose, big, spongy and covered with bright red veins which spread across fleshy cheeks. He sported a livery stable uniform of baggy coat and trousers only to be used when tending the horses in the fort. Lieutenant Halcomb frequently took him to task about it, which

Stackhouse ignored, because it was comfortable and large enough to cover his huge frame. His years in the army had taught him all about the Halcombs of the world. He reckoned him to be a pompous man with his fancy double-breasted frock coat. He was surprised he didn't wear his hat, with the cascading plumes of dyed buffalo hair, to sleep in as well. But perhaps even for the lieutenant that was a step too far.

'What we gotta go to this canyon for anyway?' Berry McChesney asked. The Irish man, who'd signed up with the army as soon as he arrived in America, worried at the spots on the back of his neck which covered the collar of his blue shirt with pus and blood.

'Injuns,' Harley Coble said. He knew about most things. People always asked him questions.

'I'm fed up wit these Injuns. Wot they doing here anyways?' McChesney muttered.

'They holing up in there according to Lieutenant Halcomb and stockpiling food, horses, anything they can lay their hands on. Army reckons if they clear them out they might stand a chance of finishing off their resistance to moving to the reservations.'

'Can't they be content with that? No government gave us land for nothing.'

McChesney was incensed by the Indians' good fortune.

'Well that ain't strictly true,' Harley Coble argued.

'Government gave land to those willing to go to Oregon for a ten dollar registration fee. And don't forget the Injuns lived on the land long before the settlers arrived. The Spanish, French and English all tried to conquer the Injuns and failed.'

'I think you've got a soft spot for those savages,' McChesney said.

'No, I'm just saying the truth of it all. The Injuns have come up short with the frontiersmen. The settlers have an army to help fight their battles 'cause the government ain't giving away land to be cultivated and just let them Injuns cause trouble.'

Berry McChesney's red hair looked as if it glowed redder. His pale green eyes, the colour of an unripe apple, were streaked red with rage.

'I think you must be an Injun lover,' he said.

The soldiers stepped back. Harley Coble was respected when it came to fighting. No one had ever counted but everyone reckoned he'd killed more Indians than anyone else. To call him an Injun lover was tantamount to calling him out. Coble's fingers twitched above his army Colt.

'Private Coble, Private McChesney, first man to draw a gun will be tied to the mouth of a cannon.'

Second Lieutenant Halcomb had entered the saloon unnoticed by the soldiers. The tension between Coble and McChesney faded and was replaced by tension between officer and men. Halcomb stared and Coble's hand moved away from his gun. He stood to attention and saluted his commander.

'A misunderstanding, sir,' he said.

'They were just having a playful discussion, sir,' Sergeant Stackhouse said.

Halcomb nodded.

'Keep the men in better order and no more discussions. Soldiers are here to follow orders, not to voice opinions.'

Halcomb was known as a hard taskmaster whom no one cared to cross. Although they weren't dragging a cannon with them they were under no illusion that he wouldn't carry out a threat once made. They'd simply continue on until they came across a fort or platoon with a cannon and the sentence would be carried out.

The men waited. They knew it was official business that Halcomb was on. He hadn't entered the saloon to join them in a drink. Officers and men didn't socialize. All were conscious of the strict layers of command. All officers held themselves apart from enlisted men. Whereas Halcomb had booked into the hotel for their stopover, the men were camped in a few tents on the edge of town. When they lived together in forts, the larger ones even had schools to educate the officers' children separately from the offspring of enlisted men. Only on the battlefield where the soldiers shared the same dangers, did they have any degree of camaraderie.

'We have a task in front of us,' Lieutenant Halcomb said.

'You mean killing Injuns in Palo Duro, sir,' Sergeant Stackhouse asked.

'We are supposed to keep that information to ourselves, Sergeant.'

The sergeant looked down at his dusty boots. 'Sorry, sir,' he mumbled.

'No, this task is one that involves the protection of the fairer sex.' Halcomb looked at his men. There were no more interruptions. 'It has come to my attention that a Mary Williamston, kidnapped as a child, is now in the hands of a half-breed Comanche. It is our duty to rescue her. I hope you are all with me on this.'

Lieutenant Halcomb couldn't have put it better to these battle-hardened soldiers. They had seen what happened to white women at the hands of renegades. The man who'd moaned about Halcomb finding them extra tasks to do didn't hesitate. He took it on himself to speak for them all.

'We're with you, Lieutenant, sir,' Bert Stackhouse said.

CHAPTER TEN

'I can understand now why you don't like the place,' she said.

Broke and Little Bluestem sat on their horses and watched from the hillside as the sun started to disappear below the horizon. The sunset washed the town with an eerie red hue. Later when they looked back, they saw the moon had now bleached the buildings to give them a starkly surreal look.

Little Bluestem was wrapped up against the bitter cold of night but she still shivered.

'I never belonged there. Never really lived there at all,' Broke said.

Little Bluestem reached across and put her hand on his arm, and as quickly pulled it back, embarrassed by her forwardness. Broke smiled.

'I'm glad you're not as young as you pretended to be,' he said.

Broke and Little Bluestem rode through the night

without stopping because they'd wasted enough time and had to put a good distance between themselves and the Comanche braves. They planned to shelter for a couple of hours at midday and give the horses a rest.

It was fall and the plains appeared to be a desert under the hot burning sky but standing between the eastern forests and the western mountains, rain could fall on parts of the land at any time. Then wild flowers, deep green grass and shallow lakes were dotted over the landscape. Now, however as Broke and Little Bluestem made their way to the mountains, the sun had sucked the earth dry. Ponds and streams dried into sand and mud and plants withered and died.

After many hours their trail led them near the Red River with its line of cottonwood trees, which they used for shelter from the burning heat. The river canyons made fertile oases. They occasionally saw wildlife, buffalo, antelope and great elk. There were cats, wolves and coyotes looking at the same things as they were, but they kept out of sight of the two humans and the three horses. Little Bluestem took the opportunity to practise her accuracy with her bow and shot a couple of small animals for the pot.

Broke studied the herds of wild horses and recalled his sturdy Appaloosa, a horse he'd tamed at the Lazy Z when he'd worked for Crosland Page. Little Bluestem had used the horse to lay a false trail.

It had been a good animal and served them to the last. Then he spotted a magnificent palomino, so blond it appeared white. He dismounted then handed his gun and arrows to Little Bluestem.

'I'm going after that,' he said.

Broke instinctively acted and thought like a horse. He'd rubbed his hands over the chestnut on his horse's inner leg to transfer a distinctive horse smell to him before he approached the palomino. He held up his hand to test the direction of the wind as he silently slipped sideways towards it. He avoided looking at the animal directly and steered clear of anything that would be interpreted by the horse as a menacing gesture. Moving to the left side of the palomino, he made soft, low, guttural noises, a special language he used for horses. Initially the animal trotted away. The colt, which Broke judged to be between two or three years old, was spirited and intelligent. Then curiosity got the better of the animal and allowed Broke to approach him again. It was going well.

Then suddenly the other horses that surrounded the colt raised their heads as if frightened. A couple of them snorted and stared. The big stallion, leader of the herd, stomped his front feet and gave a short piercing squeal. They were prey animals, ready to run if a predator came near. Broke stopped. Only sounds of soothing, murmuring reassurances came from him. Confident there was no danger around, the horses went back to grazing, and he approached again. This time he touched the colt with his fingers closed into his palm and allowed it to smell his hand. The horse didn't shy away from him and responded to light strokes on its forehead and along its nose until eventually Broke put his arms around its neck and nuzzled its face with his.

Broke fed it tidbits of roots as he encouraged the animal away from the herd. He wanted to isolate it before he made his move. The stallion would try to protect his mares and their offspring. Broke aimed to ride away and finish taming the animal as they travelled. He persuaded the colt to come near a mound of earth, to mount the animal without startling it. Before the horse was aware of what Broke meant to do, he had grabbed hold of its long mane, and held on for the inevitable rough ride. The stallion gave chase for a couple of miles, but then it gave a scream like a roar of rage, and turned back to its herd.

Broke loved the sensation of galloping wildly across the plains and yet this was tinged with sadness, as he knew that the horse would no longer be free to do this again. Memories of his own loss of freedom coloured his thoughts but only momentarily as he felt the beast beneath his body. He knew a lasting companionship would develop between them. A man who explored the western frontiers valued his horses.

Little Bluestem watched and then gathered the

reins of Broke's horse to follow him as he rode off on the palomino. The packhorse was already tied to her saddle and followed with the rest of the horses. She raced to keep up with him. She, like Broke, enjoyed a gallop and the animals, happy at the exercise, tried to keep up with the blond horse.

At first the young horse bucked and reared at leaving the herd behind, but with Broke's gentle urging it settled to a steady canter interspersed with a gallop. As soon as they were well clear of the herd, Broke placed a leather halter over its head, and although the horse shook and snorted to try and get rid of it, and its rider, Broke held tightly on to the animal. After he'd been on the horse for an hour he stopped to give all the horses a rest and to allow them to graze and water.

When he dismounted he immediately tied the colt's front leg, bent at the knee towards the pastern joint, and its hoof nearly touching its body, to keep it docile and prevent it from running back to the herd. It was a method he'd used many times before with an unruly horse, or as now, when he had little time to tame an animal. He coaxed the colt to the ground and it lay still while he brushed its coat, removing the burrs and tics, letting it to get used to his smell and touch.

Little Bluestem came near but not too close. She didn't want to frighten the horse. She made a fire and heated up some coffee and brought a cup to

Broke together with jerky to chew. She didn't want to stroke the horse – the animal had enough to get used to already – however Broke encouraged her to do so.

'You might need to hold or ride it. So it has to get to know you as well.'

Broke told her he aimed to keep the Red River to his right as they rode over the plains, and aim for the Palo Duro Canyon. The Rocky Mountains would then be within reach. The plan was to get as far away from Hell, the Comanche and anyone else who threatened to disrupt their lives. Living with the Indians had given him many skills to survive in the wilderness.

Again he watched Little Bluestem as she murmured endearments to the colt and wondered whether he ought to have left her in town. She was a white woman, no matter how much she denied it, and perhaps she ought to have the chance to experience living with her own kind.

Whenever he suggested this to her the reaction was hostile and he let the matter drop, for now.

CHAPTER ELEVEN

When Black Horse found Broke's horse and travois he showed his resentment and whipped out at the animal.

They were only chasing a squaw and an injured man yet, so far they had proved elusive. He felt he'd been made to look a fool in the eyes of the other braves and his heart was dark with thoughts of how he would make Broke suffer. A picture of Little Bluestem entered his mind, but this time she didn't invoke the usual feeling he had for her. Instead of lust, he felt only the desire to inflict pain and humiliation.

His twin brother, Wolf Slayer, hid his laughter well enough, but Black Horse could sense it bubbling under the carefully blank canvas of his face as he asked a question.

'What next, my brother?'

Black Horse kicked at the travois full of rocks and

stubbed his toe. He gritted his teeth to hide the pain. The look on his face said he would have liked to slaughter the horse, but common sense prevailed. It was a good animal.

'Untie the travois. We have to go back. If they sent the horse on to waylay us they must have holed up in those hills back there. We'll seek them out.'

The Comanche knew the land. Their people had lived here for generations. And for generations the Indians had been at war with those who wished to take their land, from the Spanish to the present day settlers. There should have been enough room for everyone, but as people started to cultivate the land, there wasn't enough left for the nomadic tribes. The difference now was that the settlers had brought an army. And they were determined to remove obstacles to colonization.

Unfortunately for Black Horse and Wolf Slayer, they refused to believe they were from a generation who knew the fight was already lost.

They arrived at the point on the trail which, in their haste to catch up with Broke and Little Bluestem, they'd missed. Black Horse, even in his rage, couldn't blame the oversight on anyone else. It had been dark when they chased after them. The frown on his face told all the other braves that he knew he should have waited until first light or perhaps not have given them so much time to escape.

It was evident from the marks on the ground that they'd succeeded reasonably well to hide the fact that it was here the pair had left the trail after loading up the rocks on to the travois to send the pursuers on a wild goose chase.

The braves followed the path the man and young woman had taken. Although Black Horse suspected they'd be long gone, he wanted to find the place they'd hidden, see if it was possible to sense which way their direction lay.

They found the cave that had earlier sheltered the pair they sought. A young brave, Shooting Star, voiced the opinion that the cave was a good place to hide out and rest. 'It's almost certain Little Bluestem found it. Broke would've been too hurt to do other than to follow,' he said.

'She will make someone a good wife,' Wolf Slayer commented.

Black Horse remained silent.

Shooting Star sat on the cave floor, using the darkness and coolness to concentrate his thoughts. Several of the elders had told him they believed he had second sight and that he ought to train his skills but so far Shooting Star rejected the notion and endeavoured to be a warrior like his brothers. But in these circumstances it was a skill worth using.

'I see a narrow dangerous trail. Below the trail are the skeletons of those who missed their footing. Their spirits linger because they haven't had the right ceremonies performed to send them to the next world. This is the direction that Broke and Little Bluestem took.'

The cave felt colder to all those who stood and listened.

'Are their spirits waiting there?' He Who Would Grow As Tall As A Mountain asked. His eyes were wide with unspoken fear. He was a fierce fighter of the living but he didn't want to challenge the dead.

'No, they haven't left this world,' Shooting Star replied.

Black Horse had little time for spirits. He was in the world of the living. 'Let's take this trail. If it's the way Broke and Little Bluestem have gone, we will continue onwards until we find them.' He told the braves what they should do. 'Fat Boy and One Who Shapes Hunting Tools, follow He Who Would Grow As Tall As A Mountain and go back along the trail with our horses. You, Sly Fox, Long Face and Rider of Horses follow us. We will make smoke signals if we find anything.'

Wolf Slayer followed his brother, accompanied by four braves, including Shooting Star, as the other three went back with the horses. In the daylight the Indians found the tracks of the fugitives. They were well hidden but even along a rocky trail, motes of dust drifted around, rocks were scuffed and small pebbles skittered down, as the pair had edged their way along the narrow ledge. Eventually they arrived at the same place where Broke had noticed the men camping at the edge of the treeline. Black Horse and Wolf Slayer made their way down the valley and told the other two braves to wait until they had found out if anyone was there.

They found the spot where Little Bluestem had spitted her attacker like a pig. Blood was all over the ground, the grass and plants flattened by feet and body.

'A bloody fight here,' Wolf Slayer observed. 'Little Bluestem?'

His brother nodded agreement. 'Broke would not have made such a mess,' he said.

They went further, cautiously keeping a watch for anything and everything, in case of trouble. Black Horse observed foot and hoofprints around the campsite. The fire, covered by the earth, was cold, the heat completely gone.

'They left here many hours ago. There were at least five, six men here,' he said. 'No one left in the camp, not even a dead body. Broke knows well the ways of the paleface and he'd take all the men to a town, alive for justice and dead for the reward.'

'The only place around here, is the town of Hell,' Wolf Slayer said.

Black Horse nodded. 'Start a fire again to make a signal to the others we need our horses. I vowed I would only let them go free if they made it to the Rocky Mountains. I don't want to break my promise.'

Once they were all together again, the braves mounted their horses and rode in the direction of Hell. It took many hours but eventually they sat on the hillside and looked at the town from their vantage point.

'Are we just going to wait here, Black Horse?'

Black Horse stared at the brave who'd asked the question. He believed that He Who Would Grow As Tall As A Mountain saw himself as a leader and there would always be competition between them. 'Do you suggest that we ride into town and attack the people? I see only nine of us here.' He spread his arms to indicate the number of warriors. 'We cannot charge into a paleface town unless it is planned. There are too many places for them to hide from us. And their guns would soon annihilate us. I will not throw my life, or yours, away on such a foolhardy venture.'

'Are you turning as feeble as a woman, Black Horse?'

Black Horse leapt off his horse and pulled the tall warrior to the floor. The youngster scrambled to his feet, his hands scrabbling at his belt to find a weapon.

Black Horse was a foot shorter but he didn't hesitate.

'No one calls me a coward and lives to repeat such a lie,' he said. His skin glistened and beads of perspiration ran down his face and chest to distort the paint on his body. The two red and black marks on his forehead and chin blurred to give him the look of a devil. He wore only a breechcloth and moccasins and feathers decorated his hair. The effect was terrifying.

'I wasn't being serious, Black Horse.'

The taller brave attempted to take back the accusation he'd made but it was too late. The look on Black Horse's face told him he might not live to regret his words. The eyes that stared at him told him he'd made a fatal mistake to accuse Black Horse of such a dishonourable thing.

They circled around each other. He Who Would Grow As Tall As A Mountain gripped his tomahawk until his knuckles turned white, while in Black Horse's hand was a broad-bladed knife he used to butcher and skin buffalo meat. He held it as if to stab downwards and the twelve-inch blade sharpened only on one side flashed as a ray of sunlight caught its surface.

Close hand-to-hand combat was unusual for the Comanche men who preferred to throw lances, shoot arrows or guns, but at this moment it seemed right. A Comanche would never step away from a battle and would fight to the death. Fighting was a religion to the warriors.

He Who Would Grow As Tall As A Mountain couldn't concentrate. Fear had leaked into his mind and made him careless. Black Horse brought the blade down and cut through his right shoulder muscle. Blood poured down his chest from the wound. He dropped his tomahawk as his hand went numb. He stepped back from another thrust and grabbed his weapon from the ground with his left hand. He slashed it through the air aiming for Black Horse's head but the brave was quick and he feinted away from the strike.

Both men were nimble on their feet and continued to circle around. He Who Would Grow As Tall As A Mountain swayed slightly as the blood loss from his arm continued. He swung his tomahawk but with the use of only one arm the grip and aim was poor. Black Horse stepped away and his opponent misjudged his aim. Black Horse avoided the blow, which would have parted his hair – permanently – and tripped his opponent over. He followed him to the ground and brought the knife down and this time he stabbed and slashed open He Who Would Grow As Tall As A Mountain's chest, crunching the rib bones and exposing the heart. He had no need to make another stab. He watched as the young brave's heart slowed and then stopped.

No one spoke for a moment. There was nothing to say. Black Horse had proved his strength and bravery. He Who Would Grow As Tall As A Mountain was dead. Nevertheless Black Horse's heart was heavy and filled with sorrow. His family had lost a warrior, hunter and provider. Too late he recalled his father's warning and the taboo of killing one's own.

Black Horse wanted to follow Broke and Little Bluestem immediately and get away from his foolhardy actions but he could not ignore the Comanche tradition to place the dead brave to rest in the traditional way.

Wolf Slayer helped Black Horse get him ready. They brought the young warrior's knees up, placed his arms over his chest and bent his head forward to make the body as compact as possible.

'Do we send his horse with him as well, Black Horse?' Shooting Star asked.

He nodded. 'We have to make his passage to the happy hunting grounds as easy as possible.'

Black Horse killed the horse by the deft use of his knife. Two braves found a place where He Who Would Grow As Tall As A Mountain could be safely put to rest. His weapons were broken, and then, together with his saddle and horse, were placed by his side.

They renamed him as they covered his body, He Who Would Never Grow As Tall As A Mountain.

CHAPTER TWELVE

It had been a bad few weeks in Hell, but Marshal Jones was pleased to have law and order back again. The outlaws were locked up and waiting for the circuit judge. Broke and his white squaw were gone; the soldiers were packing up to move out. All was well.

The judge was due in town in the next couple of days and the Nixon gang would be on trial for robbery and murder. The noose was ready because it didn't take long for the men of Hell to build a gallows. The gang had killed a woman who'd tried to snatch her purse back. It would be a short trial.

If the marshal had a list of people to blame for the trouble he'd surely place Broke at the top. 'That man Broke is nothing but a nuisance. Until he came to town, Hell wasn't an unpleasant place to be,' he mumbled.

Deputy Wills, sitting in the law office, agreed. 'He

has a bad effect on folks. Why, even that Maisy Martin helped him to escape from jail.' The youngster spat on his badge and polished it against his waistcoat. 'I'll make sure it's all peaceful again outside,' he said.

Marshal Jones watched his deputy leave then put his booted feet on the desk and relaxed. He reached down for the bottle of medicinal whiskey in the drawer and forgot that Broke had in fact made Hell a better place.

The lawman knocked back another slug of whiskey. He'd been worried that Broke would find out the gang had harmed Lizbeth with a ricocheted bullet. Although it was Mrs Payette who'd been killed as she tried to protect her savings, there'd be a whole deal of trouble because Lizbeth was involved. The marshal reckoned nothing would stop him from tearing the men apart, slowly, limb from limb to get vengeance. He tipped yet another slug of the medicinal drink down his throat and shuddered at the same time. As he coughed he cursed Broke.

'Did that boy no good spending all those years with the Comanche,' he muttered.

Only the prisoners in the cells heard him and they didn't disagree.

Later, after a short sleep, and being woken by Don Wills to report everything quiet before he went out again, Marshal Jones sat up, stretched and decided to take a look-see for himself. He needed to exercise his creaky bones. No one was going to spring the prisoners. Everyone in town wanted a hanging and the excuse for a shindig. No doubt he'd see Deputy Wills in the Last Chance Saloon, or one of the new saloons, which he reckoned opened every week. As far as he was concerned Don Wills was too fond of gambling to go and look for any trouble so Jones liked to check up one last time before retiring for the night.

He stood in front of his mirror and brushed his hair. Not that he had much hair to boast about, which was another thing he blamed Broke for. When Broke first came to town, Marshal Jones's hair turned metallic grey. Since his second visit he reckoned there were more hairs on his moustache and in the comb than on his head. He didn't think it would survive a third call from Broke.

For a moment Marshal Jones experienced the odd sensation of being observed that made the few hairs he had at the back of his neck stand up and his skin prickle. He quickly turned round, peered into the gloom but couldn't see anything. He took the silver glass off the wall and examined it. The back was peeling. He replaced it.

'Need a dang new mirror,' he said.

However it unnerved him enough to pour himself just one more medicinal whiskey. He decided he'd best stay in his office to watch the prisoners after all. And after yet another glass, he edged towards the mirror again to make sure the apparition was just an illusion.

Had Marshal Jones had been aware of his visitor he'd have figured out that similar thoughts about the lack of hair flowed through Black Horse's mind.

The Indian had slipped in unseen like a shadow when Deputy Wills had opened the door to go out and make his rounds of the town again. He'd stood still and unnoticed by the two lawmen. The only one to see him was Doady Nixon, who watched and waited for what would happen next.

The shadow moved and before Marshal Jones had time to call out 'Who's there?' or grab the shotgun from his desk, Black Horse had his arm around his throat, and a tomahawk pressed against his forehead.

'Where's Broke? The man you call Mitch Bayfield, where is he?' The marshal could hardly choke the words out from the stranglehold but the feel of the tomahawk made lots of things possible.

'He's gone. Went with that squaw after he'd brought the outlaws here.'

'How long ago did he leave?'

'Last night and if you're after him you'd best be off fast 'cause he's got the US Cavalry going after him as well.' Black Horse eased his hold on the marshal's neck to encourage him to continue talking. 'Seems they're out to rescue the squaw, I mean a white gal, from Broke.'

The marshal, had he not been in such a bad situation, might have laughed at the irony of it. No one had rescued Mitch Bayfield from the Indians.

'Which direction did they take?'

'They went across the plains. That's all I know.'

Marshal Jones knew nothing more for a while: Black Horse smashed his tomahawk on the lawman's head. He left him his scalp, such as it was.

Doady Nixon, seeing the marshal out cold, took a chance to call out to the Indian. He knew it was a long shot. The Indian could either ignore him or scalp him, but as he was facing a hanging party soon, he reckoned it didn't make much difference.

'You, yes you, Injun,' Doady Nixon shouted. 'How about you throw us the keys, and we won't make a noise and let everyone know about you hitting the marshal?'

Black Horse looked across at the outlaws. He didn't care whether the outlaws yelled or not because he could slip out as silently as he'd got in and disappear as quickly. But it did amused him to cause as much mayhem as possible. Without saying a word, he took the keys from the marshal's belt, threw them into the cells and left without a backwards glance.

Doady Nixon couldn't believe his luck.

He knew the Indian could have just as easy ignored him. He picked up the keys from the floor and felt the strong iron metal with his fingers. Walter Minke moaned in his sleep but Roland Lang stirred and rolled over on the bunk. He could hear nothing from Todd or Palo. Doady weighed up the situation. Tomorrow, or the next day they'd all end up as cottonwood blossom. Andy Pope was already singing with the angels, or more likely stoking furnaces down below, so he wouldn't be suffering the pain of having his neck stretched and broken, no one would put a necktie on him. Only thing to consider, briefly, was the rest of the gang: they'd slow him down. He was going on his own.

Doady's hand shook as he tried each key in the lock. Eventually he found the right one and turned it. The door opened. He couldn't stay any longer. The marshal might be out cold but the deputy could return any moment. Before Doady could get out, Roland was by his side.

'What ye doing, Doady? How d'you get those keys?'

'You comin', or you gonna ask questions?'

'Shall I wake the others? An' what about Walter? An' Todd? Can't leave them here to die.'

'If we drag Walter and Todd with us, they'll hold us up and we'll all die. If they can crawl out the cell unaided, well, OK.'

Roland shook Walter, Todd and Palo. Walter was ready to move instantly. The chance of escaping a hanging galvanized the injured man to action and he was as jumpy as a long-tailed cat in a room full of rocking chairs. Todd moaned and groaned with the pain of his arm, but he wasn't staying behind either.

Doady didn't wait to find out what Roland or the rest were up to. He used a key to open the gun cupboard and helped himself to guns and ammunition. He turned and threw a rifle to Roland who'd followed him into the room a few seconds later.

'They got some good Winchesters here.' Doady grabbed a couple of Colt .45s. 'Take one of these as well.'

Walter armed himself with a Remington and loaded it. Doady reckoned he looked sick enough to frighten the dogs from a gut wagon but figured as long as he could put one foot in front of the other he'd let him trail along. Fortunately Todd wasn't a bad shot with his left hand as well as his right but chose a pistol rather than a heavy rifle.

Doady elbowed the men back from the door. 'Folks might notice all five of us rushing out so we'll creep out, one at a time. I got the keys so I get to go first. We'll meet at the livery stables.'

There was no one around: all the good folks were tucked into their beds and the rest filled the saloons. A shout went up from the Last Chance Saloon as Deputy Don Wills bluffed on ten high for the pot and ordered another glass of beer to celebrate, and everywhere the noise of out of tune honky-tonk pianos filled the air. There was no one to notice shadows flitting along the street and going into Bayfield's livery stables. A few people might have stirred in their slumbers as the horses rode out of town, but the stable boy wouldn't tell the townsfolk anything as he sat slumped on a bale of hay with his head staved in by the butt of a gun.

'Where we heading, Doady?' Roland asked. 'We gonna go after that half-breed who brought us in?'

'The half-breed has a band of Comanche after him, plus I heard the army want the white squaw he's got tagging along with him. Whatever the truth of it he'll have a whole pile of trouble on his heels. One of them is bound to finish him off so I'm voting we head off to New Mexico and disappear.'

CHAPTER THIRTEEN

The soldiers finally packed up camp to leave town at midday. Marshalling a troop of men in some sort of order wasn't easy when they'd filled themselves with the local whiskey 'til they were drunk.

Lieutenant Halcomb was further delayed after he heard news of a rumpus during the night. He felt honour bound to investigate before he left.

'Don't know what happened,' the spotty-faced and exceedingly hung-over deputy sat with his elbows on the marshal's desk. He rested his head in his hands and moaned. 'I was out doing the rounds and went in the saloon for a drink' – he looked up at the lieutenant as if expecting a challenge – ' 'cause I was thirsty, and then, couldn't have been more than a half hour, I came back to find the marshal with his head bashed in an' seeing stars and the prisoners escaped.'

Lieutenant Halcomb looked around the law office.

'The cell isn't broken open. I believe the keys are kept on the marshal's belt. Someone must've helped the prisoners.' Deputy Wills's eyes were red from drink and lack of sleep. They were qualities that didn't aid his assumptions. 'That half-breed Injun must've come back for them.'

'I don't think he would've brought them in here just to break them out again,' Lieutenant Halcomb observed.

'He might if he found out they'd hurt Miss Lizbeth. Talk is they were once sparking.'

The lieutenant frowned.

'Is the marshal OK?'

'Doc's with him now.' Deputy Wills smiled broadly. 'It looks like I might be made up to marshal.'

Lieutenant Halcomb raised his eyebrows. 'I'll keep my eyes open. If I find them I'll hang all of them. Save you a whole deal of trouble.'

The troop followed the route Broke and the girl had taken earlier.

'I don't know what the Indian is up to,' Lieutenant Halcomb said. 'There are lots of hoofprints going out of town but it don't mean they're all travelling together. We'll stick with the original plan to get the girl and if we find these bank robbers, we'll hang them. I'll make a report when we get back to Fort Concho.'

'Do you think he and the girl are heading for the Pecos?' Stackhouse asked. He stroked the fuzzy beard he'd started to grow as winter reared its ugly head and the weather started to chill in the early mornings and evening. 'That sure is rough country out there.'

'Don't think he'll take that route,' Lieutenant Halcomb said. 'He will want to get as far away as possible, perhaps hole up in the mountains. He'd make his way to the Rocky Mountains and the easiest route is to keep the Red River to his right and aim for the Palo Duro Canyon.'

'Ain't that just where we gotta to go?'

Lieutenant Halcomb smiled from ear to ear. 'Turns out we might be able to scoop up everything in one go. I have a notion that he doesn't know he's doing us a good turn.'

'Yeah, you're right, sir,' Stackhouse agreed.

'Since Marshal Jones reckoned the man's out of favor with the Comanche, he might not know that a whole darn band of them are in the canyon. He won't know which way to turn when he sees them and then finds we are up his backside.'

The soldiers stared with incredulity as their officer laughed with delight – it was a thing rarely witnessed, least of all by his own men.

The small troop of forty men and horses, with its one wagon, snaked in a ragged line across the plains. They made a cacophony of sounds – men on a march

– as cups rattled against skillets on their backpacks and the leather saddles creaked together with the grinding of iron wagon wheels.

Lieutenant Halcomb was a tough leader. He'd been known to force his men to ride a punishing sixty miles a day. Today they had a lighter step in their journey. Today at least they knew where they were going and who they were after. It wasn't always like that because if they were told to follow an officer they were trained to follow commands without protest.

Bert Stackhouse took a sip of whiskey from his water container to ease his aching bones. He was well past the age to be a soldier but had reached the stage where there was no other profession open to him. He could ride but he couldn't tell one end of a cow from another unless it mooed, so he reckoned ranch work would throw up a whole lot of problems. He once had a notion about farming but unfortunately every plant he'd ever touched wilted under his not-so-green fingers.

He had even deserted from the army fifteen years ago and tried his hand at being a marshal. He shook his head to clear the image of him quaking in his boots as every gunslinger came to town to play 'let's shoot the new marshal' until he finally decided the army was the better option.

When he rejoined he didn't even bother to change his name like other deserters did. He'd heard they were desperate for men in the Civil War – why, they even took slaves into the army, although they had their own regiments. It kept things in some sort of order that way, he guessed.

Coming out of his musings about the past, Stackhouse had another thought. 'What we gonna do with this woman when we rescue her from the Comanche?' he asked.

He rode behind Lieutenant Halcomb and near to Private Paul Gregoire, but it was Private Dewry Hembree further down the line who answered.

'I'll escort her to safety,' he said. He licked his lips at the vision that came into his head and his eyes glazed.

Private Isaac Colwell laughed. He and Hembree were the closest you got to mates in the army. They even talked about going into partnership after they left the service, although the details were vague. They'd signed up for seven years after going on a bender on a night's leave from a cattle trail. They both said they'd had enough of the stink of cattle, and eating dust and flies. Colwell spat the plains dust from his throat and a glob of brown phlegm hit the ground.

'We'd make sure she appreciates white men after suffering Comanche,' he said. The comments were aimed at Hembree but everyone heard his words.

'Yeah, I'm sure she'll find out what she's missing after a spell with you and Hembree,' Gregoire said.

'She'd beg us to give her back to the Injuns.'

'You saying we don't know how to treat a lady?' Colwell asked. He had the scowl of a mean, aggressive man.

Gregoire looked at the tall thin man whose legs almost dragged along the ground. Colwell hadn't got one ounce of extra flesh but that didn't do him any favours because he looked like an ugly bag of bones. Gregoire always said Stackhouse should've shared a couple of hundred pounds of his surplus flesh with Colwell and that way they could have a decent body each.

'I ain't saying anything like that. Never seen you with a lady, that's all. I hear most of those women from the cribs are blind who take to you.'

'Take those words back, Gregoire.' Colwell shouted along the line again. His gun cleared leather ready to shoot.

Unfortunately for Colwell, Lieutenant Halcomb heard the threats. Usually immune to the men's rambling, rough conversations, he couldn't avoid interfering when discipline was threatened. He turned slightly in the saddle and shouted at his men.

'Silence in the ranks, and if anyone else draws a gun without my say so, they'll be shot.'

Although there were a few low grumbles for a couple of minutes, the soldiers did as ordered.

Lieutenant Halcomb turned forward and spurred his horse into a gallop. A faster pace might discourage the men from their habit of engaging in useless chat. Occasionally over the next few hours he looked behind him to check that his men weren't at each other's throats. That Sergeant Stackhouse wore stable clothes for comfort hadn't gone unnoticed but was ignored by the lieutenant, as an army great coat now covered the inappropriate uniform. It had the unfortunate effect of making him sweat which, with the booze he had consumed, made the man stink like a saloon.

'I can't see that young couple, Lieutenant,' Sergeant Stackhouse said. 'We should've had them in our sights by now.'

'We shouldn't have rested so long in Hell,' Lieutenant Halcomb said. His irritation surfaced like a lump of bile at the back of his throat. He swallowed the temper that threatened to explode. That young deputy and his incoherent ramblings had delayed him for far too long. He reckoned the townsfolk would soon find out Don Wills wore a ten-dollar Stetson on a five-cents head.

They continued to make their way to Palo Duro Canyon and, with no further sign of the pair, Halcomb, as much as he wanted to 'rescue' Mary Williamston, knew, ultimately, he couldn't let it interfere with his duty. Then his luck turned. Sergeant Stackhouse picked up some tracks.

'Looks like they're heading a little west of our destination, sir.'

Halcomb gritted his teeth. He had to make a tough decision. It had been easy while he only had to trail them towards the canyon. He dismounted and paced around for a few minutes.

'It's not too far off track,' he said. Then he turned to his sergeant, 'Stackhouse, take twenty-five men to the canyon and I'll take the rest with me to find the girl. That man can't be allowed to keep her. We can go after the girl and then go to the aid of the colonel.'

'Are you sure, sir?'

The soldiers didn't often take the risk of questioning an order, but with a few extra swigs of whiskey inside him to give him courage, Stackhouse voiced the opinion that if Colonel Mackenzie had requested extra men, then he needed extra men.

Lieutenant Halcomb's reply was laced with fury. 'Don't dare question me, Sergeant,' he shouted. 'We can't let him get away with taking the girl. I'm sure Colonel Mackenzie will agree.'

The sergeant shrugged his shoulders in a manner that described his feelings. It wasn't his head on the block so if the fool wanted to play the hero, and fail, there wasn't anything he could do about it.

'Yes, sir,' he said.

Earlier, Halcomb's temper would have been short enough to draw on Stackhouse, but now he mulled over how well the whole situation had played into his hands. He was following his orders to the letter, along with the soldiers from forts dotted all over the plains, to keep the settlers safe and to help Colonel Ranald S. Mackenzie. The colonel with his 4th US Cavalry was set to trap the whole caboodle of Indians in their hideout. A look of satisfaction appeared on his face as he rode along at the head of his reduced troop of men and imagined the medals being pinned to his uniform by his commanding officer's attractive daughter.

He'd been in the army for six years and promotion had been rapid. He was the son of a colonel and had much to prove. It was all going well as far as he was concerned.

Lieutenant Halcomb took fifteen men with him who, resigned to their fate, fell in after him. He kept at a brisk canter to cover the miles without tiring the horses too much and it gave him time to reflect on his future. Second Lieutenant Rodger Halcomb felt satisfied about the glory of not only being involved in the campaign, but also rescuing a damsel in distress.

CHAPTER FOURTEEN

Black Horse followed Broke's trail for several miles. What he surmised disturbed him: it looked as if Broke was leading the soldiers to Palo Duro Canyon to betray them.

For months the Comanche, Cheyenne and Kiowa had stashed supplies for a last stand against the pale-faces. It was their 'safe haven'. The canyon also held over 1,500 horses.

The idea of stockpiling had been mooted before Broke left the encampment. Whatever was true, the soldiers were following Broke and chance might lead them there. Black Horse's idea was to find Broke before he led the army to Palo Duro and to safeguard the Indians.

He turned his horse and joined the rest of the Comanche band.

'Is Broke definitely heading for there?' Wolf Slayer asked. He looked puzzled. 'Why would he lead the soldiers towards the Comanche stockpile? I'd never believe that Broke could betray us like this. Perhaps we were wrong to let him go?'

'It is done,' Black Horse said. 'We are lucky to have a head start on the soldiers and we can stop Broke's treachery.'

The group of braves continued to follow the tracks of the two riders, and the soldiers, determined to catch up with them.

In turn Broke and Little Bluestem wasted no time crossing the plains. They rarely stopped apart from short rests for the horses. They had several nights' start on the Comanche, but Broke knew Black Horse would soon make up the distance between them. The Indians were excellent horsemen. They covered miles in a more disciplined manner than any army.

Once they reached the Rocky Mountains he and Little Bluestem would be safe but it seemed a long way off. As they passed the outskirts of the Lazy Z Ranch, he did think of calling on Crosland Page, but decided that the people and places belonged to the past. Lou Neal had assured him that Lizbeth had only suffered a graze and Gil Tander had made no mention of it so he decided to let the matter rest.

They rode as fast as the wind and made good progress even though at times the packhorse slowed

the pace. Broke rode the palomino, the strong-spir-
ited colt enjoying a fast gallop. He sat on its back with
a blanket between the horse and himself, leather
reins over its head and a gentle bit in its mouth.

Broke had no idea that Lieutenant Halcomb was
on their tail, although he was aware they were being
followed. Once, when they stopped, he put an ear to
the ground and was surprised by the multitude of
vibrations that shook the earth. He told Little
Bluestem, 'It sounds as if the whole of the Comanche
Nation is after us.'

'So they've nearly caught up with us!' Little
Bluestem cried. Her face contorted with the fear she
felt.

They raced onwards again but, as Little Bluestem
looked back, she saw them. The dust betrayed their
presence. Broke slowed his horse to a halt. For miles
the plains undulated before them. There might be
places to hide, a nook, a swell, a mirage where the
eyes were deceived for a while. Broke dismounted
and hitched the colt with its reins tied to a small rock
that he pushed into the ground. Little Bluestem did
the same with her horse.

'Why are we stopping?' she asked. 'We have little
time to escape.'

'We have to face them,' he said. 'There is nowhere
to flee.'

'I don't want to, Broke. You'll be killed if we stay,'
she said.

'The confrontation is inevitable,' Broke said. 'There has been bad feeling since I left the Comanche band after the death of Beautiful.'

Little Bluestem interrupted, 'Black Horse and Wolf Slayer are as warriors now.'

Broke gave Little Bluestem a wry smile. 'I think I am big enough to fight them,' he said.

'I didn't mean . . .' Little Bluestem flushed red with embarrassment. 'I mean . . . I don't want you to get hurt again.'

He put his arm around her shoulders. 'When I went into the Comanche camp after a year's absence I wasn't ready for what was bound to happen between Black Horse and me. This time it will be different.'

He watched as they drew close and then halted. Black Horse, Wolf Slayer and the other braves were only a short distance away and Broke made his way towards them. Before he went he told Little Bluestem to wait with the horses but if things started to look bad to take the young colt and ride like the wind towards the safety of the mountains.

'They won't want to chase after you,' Broke said. 'If I'm killed that should be victory enough.' Little Bluestem reached up and put her arms around him. She kissed him.

'What was that for?' he smiled.

'For luck,' she said.

Everyone knew it was a fight between Broke and Black Horse.

There had been bad blood between the two since Broke had left the Comanche. The twins told Broke they considered him to be a brother and couldn't understand his desire to find his family. As far as they were concerned the Comanche *were* his family. Although Broke had tried to tell them many times that he thought no less of them, feelings now ran high between the brothers.

Broke halted and waited for Black Horse to dismount. He watched the brave throw the reins to his brother, Wolf Slayer, and turn to face him.

'So you didn't make it to the mountains?' Black Horse didn't wait for an answer. 'You know that this is the end of the trail for you? The only path you will follow is to the happy hunting grounds.'

'It might be you to take that path first, Black Horse.'

To the Indians, fighting was taking the enemy unawares, picking them off one by one or skilful battles waged on horseback. This time Broke and Black Horse faced each other as equals. Broke had a natural skill for fighting but he stabbed his Bowie knife into the ground.

'I don't want to fight you, Black Horse. You are my brother.'

The braves, and Little Bluestem who had ignored Broke's advice to stay back, made a circle and surrounded the two men as they waited for Black Horse's reply. Broke, stripped down to his breech-cloth, showed how Little Bluestem's healing hands, and the potions she'd administered, had worked well. The scars across his chest would never completely fade and told their own story of his bravery under torture.

Black Horse equalled the man in front of him in height and build even though years and experience were on Broke's side.

'You want to stand there and allow me to kill you?'

'Surely there has been enough fighting between us.'

'It will not be over until one of us is dead.'

Black Horse raised his tomahawk.

'This is madness,' Little Bluestem cried out.

Momentarily the men paused and Black Horse said to Broke, 'Looks as if you've already taught her the ways of white women. They always interfere too much.'

'No, you're wrong,' she answered for Broke. 'You are like brothers and here you are fighting one another again.'

'That brother,' Black Horse spat out the words, 'has betrayed me and the whole of the Comanche people.'

Broke stood tall. He couldn't let it pass without defending himself.

'I have not betrayed you. I don't know anything to betray you about.'

'Don't tell me you do not know the soldiers are after you?'

Broke shook his head. 'I had no idea.'

'We had to take a different path to catch up with you and overtake the soldiers who are following you and Little Bluestem.'

'I promise you, I had no knowledge of this,' Broke said.

'You are here, not a mile from Palo Duro Canyon, and you claim ignorance? You are leading the army to where the Comanche, Cheyenne and Kiowa are preparing to fight the palefaces.' He stood tall and proud as he voiced the next words. 'And we will win.'

'Black Horse, there is no battle to win. You, we, have lost the war. The Indians have been forced onto reservations and the Treaties have been broken. But whatever I believe I would never be disloyal to you. Let us be friends.'

'Our elders have lost their taste for war, but we, the young, are not ready to play dead. To the Comanche to live is to fight. There is no reason to be alive other than to conquer the enemy,' Black Horse said. 'And this battle between us I will win.'

He threw the tomahawk at Broke.

Only Broke's quick-wittedness saved him. He heard the sound, rather than saw the weapon come towards him and he ducked. It whizzed past and missed his head by less than an inch. Broke rushed at Black Horse and head-butted him. He sent him flying backwards on to the ground, took advantage of his plight and went after him. Black Horse was hard to pin to the ground, his body smothered with bear grease afforded no grip, and he sent Broke flying over the top of him. Broke rolled with the fall and both were on their feet in a matter of seconds. Broke appealed to Black Horse once again but the young brave refused to give in.

Black Horse took a tomahawk from another brave and came at Broke. Little Bluestem pulled Broke's knife from the ground and threw it towards him. He caught it deftly before Black Horse had time to wield his hatchet. Broke used the knife to take the tomahawk from his grasp with a well-aimed throw. Black Horse yelled with pain and fury as the bone in his wrist cracked. Broke followed through by racing towards Black Horse, but this time he made sure he held him, bear grease or no, in a neck lock and pulled his head back.

Broke scooped up the knife and used it to threaten Black Horse. 'I want to end this fight between us,' he said. 'Let Little Bluestem chose her own destiny. Remember she is like me.' Broke gestured towards the girl. 'She doesn't belong anywhere.'

'I vowed to kill you if I found you before you reached the Rocky Mountains.' Black Horse was stubborn and still spoiling for the fight to continue despite the knife at his throat.

'I don't think you are in the same bargaining position as before,' Broke said. He pulled at Black

129

Horse's hair. 'I don't want to kill you, but if need be I will scalp you so you never go to the Happy Hunting Ground, whatever else you do in the future.'

He knew Black Horse wouldn't want this to happen. His shame would be there for all to see. He wouldn't be able to do all the things a brave warrior should do.

'I can see the Rocky Mountains from here,' Wolf Slayer said.

Broke eased his hold on Black Horse and spoke to the two brothers. 'Can I help you fight off the soldiers?' he asked. 'I didn't bring them here intentionally.'

Black Horse had known Broke all his life and looked up to the paleface who'd taken the Comanche ways in his stride. A man he'd admired as a boy. His ire was spent with the torture already inflicted on Broke, the death of He Who Would Grow As Tall As A Mountain, and now this fight.

'Let's halt our quarrel at least until after the soldiers have been driven away,' he said.

Broke nodded agreement. He was in a superior position but he was big enough to allow the young brave to take the lead. Black Horse tied a leather thong around his broken wrist for support. He didn't show his pain.

He was a warrior.

CHAPTER FIFTEEN

The cavalry weren't known for silence, in fact those they came to help, often hailed the noise of their approach with shouts of encouragement and relief. Their horse's hoofs pounded the hard ground and the dust sent a signal to Broke and the braves that they were on their way.

The Comanche disappeared. They had moved on from the place where Broke and Black Horse had confronted one another. They found a place to ambush the soldiers. A bullet or an arrow waited for each one of them.

Second Lieutenant Halcomb eased his horse to a trot.

There was nothing obvious to give an indication that they were near the girl and the half-breed Indian but Halcomb whispered to the soldier at his side that he sensed something slightly out of kilter with the rest of the landscape. He noticed the broken blades of grass and the snapped twigs, which marked the path of their quarry.

'I want you eight men to stop here and wait for the bugle to sound,' he said. 'The rest of us will ride forward and investigate.'

He gave nothing more away in words or gestures as he led the soldiers onwards. They rode fast and hard until suddenly the Indians stepped out from the cover and surrounded them.

He was surprised to see Broke with the Indians who were said to be chasing him.

'I see you are with your own kind again,' the lieutenant said to Broke.

'Better than to be with your kind,' he answered.

It was a tense atmosphere. The soldiers looked round unsure how many Indians were hidden in the trees. A young doe flew from the bushes and startled the men. Gregoire blew the bugle at a signal from the lieutenant. In a panic, McChesney fired his gun without waiting for the order but before the bullet left the barrel he was dead. His shot went wild and the bullet embedded itself into the tree beyond as an arrow pierced his eye.

The other horses reared and turned around uncontrollably and the soldiers fought to get them back under control. In the skirmish Gregoire, Coble and the youngster Syd Turnkey were brought down as they tried to fire their rifles. They were dead as they hit the ground. One soldier tried to flee but his back was peppered with arrows as soon as he turned his horse. The three other soldiers who had ridden in with the lieutenant refused to obey his order to fight on and threw down their rifles and handguns.

The fight was over.

'I only came for the girl,' Lieutenant Halcomb cried out amidst the chaos. 'I'll give you guns and firewater in exchange for her.'

It was against army policy to trade firearms and whiskey with the Indians but he decided in the circumstances it was the politic thing to do. The Indians listened to him and then laughed.

'We have plenty of guns now,' Wolf Slayer said. 'Yours. And the girl stays here.'

The lieutenant raged, 'Mary Williamston is a white girl who should not live among savages.'

Little Bluestem stepped forward.

'Will somebody ask me what I want?'

The lieutenant's face said it all. He wasn't interested. It was merely the principle of the thing. To him everyone had a place where they belonged and once that line was blurred it became a difficult situation to deal with.

Then all hell broke loose.

Halcomb hadn't reached the rank of second lieutenant through his sweet personality: he was known to have a good command of strategic skills. At a signal from him the eight soldiers, who'd been ordered to stay back, now attacked. The 'surrendered' soldiers retrieved their guns and fired on the Indians.

Most of the young braves were armed only with tomahawks and bows and arrows. Only Wolf Slayer and Broke sported guns. Wolf Slayer fired his Remington rifle, his prized weapon stolen from a homestead, and Broke used his Henry rifle, but all too late.

Guns blazed on both sides and the surprise of the attack allowed Lieutenant Halcomb to swoop down, grab the girl, and haul her to his saddle. Everything happened so quickly she had no time to resist. His spurs gouged into the sides of his horse and he rode off.

It was over as soon as it began and once the lieutenant had the girl, the soldiers followed. Before Broke and the other braves had time to take in what had happened in the few brief moments of the fight, Wolf Slayer was wounded and his twin brother Black Horse, dead. A bullet had found its way to his throat as he screamed out his battle cry. Fat Boy breathed his last. Rider of Horses suffered a bullet wound to his leg. Only Shooting Star, Sly Fox, Long Face and One Who Shapes Hunting Tools remained unhurt.

'Little Bluestem has been taken by the soldiers,' Sly Fox said.

To Broke that wasn't as important as the events before him. Little Bluestem wouldn't be killed. That wasn't the aim of the soldiers. They merely sought to rescue a white maiden from red savages. The brother he'd known for a long time was dead and another lay wounded. The bullet was in Wolf Slayer's chest. Broke listened to the beat of his heart. It was slow and steady and in Broke's estimation his strength warranted the risk of digging the bullet from his chest. It was now the right time to do it. The young brave slipped in and out of consciousness so it would be less painful for him. The braves made a small fire while Broke inserted the blade, sliced the flesh and gouged out the bullet. He sealed the wound with a knife that had been heated until it glowed red. The smell of burnt flesh wafted under his nose.

'We will kill those soldiers for this outrage,' Shooting Star vowed.

Broke tied a strip of soft buffalo hide over the wound once he was sure it was clean.

'You will need to get Wolf Slayer to where he can rest,' he said. 'And then take his brother Black Horse home to his resting place. His father would want that.'

'Home?' Long Face queried. 'And where might that be? Is it on the reservation where the soldiers have forced us to go? Or on the plains where the settlers have taken over our land?'

The other braves agreed with him. They were full of despair at the way their people had been treated. Broke wondered if the fight between the palefaces and the Indians would ever end.

'We are nearer to the Palo Duro Canyon. Perhaps

we can take our brothers there?' Broke suggested.

The canyon was a good place to hide. It was in the midst of the plains, a huge crater hidden by an apparently flat landscape. It wasn't visible until almost at its rim, yet it was one of the biggest canyons they knew. The Indians were attracted to the canyon by the waters of the Prairie Dog Town fork of the Red River, there was ample game, edible plants and protection from the weather the canyon afforded.

A Comanche warrior, known as Red Warbonnet, stood on the rim of the crater and looked around. The majority of Indians had accepted their lot but there were many who wanted to fight on, regain their lands. He was taking his turn to scout for the tribes who planned to make a final stand. Red Warbonnet used his knife to shape an ash wood bow to pass the hours. His thoughts went back to the time he would have been able to watch the buffalo travelling like the waves of a dark-brown ocean as they made their way grazing on the thick grasses, a herd so large it would have taken a rider a week to travel from one end to the other. Now things had changed and the paleface's cattle stood in their place.

There were trails across the plains that took thousands of cattle towards the iron horses and onwards to the markets in the east and north. Red Warbonnet had seen the changes with his own eyes and no matter how much his people tried to destroy the iron tracks, it made no difference. They were replaced and cattle were transported again. Only a few thousand of the noble beasts survived as the settlers slaughtered the buffalo to make room for their own cattle.

But things would change back again; of this Comanche warrior Red Warbonnet was certain. He told the young men that the Comanche, Kiowa and Cheyenne were going to strike back. The braves were ready to listen. At first the Indians had welcomed the settlers and said the country was big enough for everyone; however, the palefaces wanted it all and pushed them off their lands. The Indians made treaties with the white chiefs but the army broke its promises.

The warriors' idea of gathering together enough horses, food, and weapons to enable them to fight and regain their lands was a good one, he reckoned, and he looked back into the canyon and saw a herd of nearly 2,000 horses. Many families had already moved here and the whole place looked like a giant encampment.

His thoughts turned to the present as he noticed something in the distance. He didn't alert anyone, just hunkered down to watch and wait. Too late, Red Warbonnet saw how many US soldiers had amassed; too late he fired off a warning shot.

Eight columns of the 4th US Cavalry and five companies of the 10th and 11th Infantry had arrived at the canyon. They, together with an assortment of scouts including Seminole, Lipan Apache and Tonkawa Indians were ready to fight. The military expedition led by Colonel Ranald S. Mackenzie had been sent to remove the Indians to reservations in Oklahoma. One of Mackenzie's scouts had found the Indian camp and notified the colonel. He sent out for reinforcements. As the soldiers looked down they saw a burning, seething cauldron of activity, filled with the dramatic light and colour of thousands of people and horses.

The Indians' control of the canyon was about to change.

CHAPTER SIXTEEN

Now, on the morning of 28 September 1874, the United States Cavalry was at the edge of the canyon and the officers were discussing how to attack.

'Can anyone see a place to get down to those Indians and rout them out?' Mackenzie asked.

Lieutenant Polk of the 11th Infantry shook his head. 'Looks like they've got an impenetrable spot.'

Mackenzie's lips drew into a thin, hard line. 'That sort of attitude loses battles for us. We're here and there is no turning back.'

'There's thousands of the redskins down there,' Sergeant Fume of the 3rd Company of the 10th Infantry commented. 'And half of them are women and children.'

'Next man who finds a reason not to fight will be court martialled.'

There were no more comments on the subject.

'Another company has arrived, sir,' Sergeant Fume said.

Mackenzie rose in his saddle and stared at the straggly troop of twenty-five men coming along the path to meet them.

'Colonel Mackenzie, sir.' Sergeant Stackhouse saluted then introduced himself. 'I'm Sergeant Stackhouse of the 4th Company to join you, sir.'

'Is this all Colonel Maslow could spare?'

Sergeant Stackhouse squirmed uncomfortably in his saddle.

'Second Lieutenant Halcomb will be along shortly with fifteen extra men, Sir. He's gone to rescue a white girl kidnapped by the Comanche.'

Colonel Mackenzie's men feared for their officer's health as they watched the veins in his forehead and neck plump up and his face turn the colour of an over-ripe eggplant. He looked as if he was about to explode. Then the moment passed, but from experience everyone knew this wouldn't be the end of the matter.

A moment later there was a more serious distraction. An Indian was seen to lift his rifle to fire a warning. An accurate shot from a Tonkawa Indian scout quickly dispatched him.

'What do we do now, sir?'

'We fight them.'

'Which way down, sir?'

There was no obvious way down, but nothing

would stop the determined colonel. He didn't hesitate. Now the Indians were aware of their presence they had to attack.

'Over the top, men!'

The colonel blazed the trail as he led the way down the steep sides of the canyon. The men followed. They looked magnificent, dressed in blue, and presented as a torrent of water cascading over the side of a mountain. The charge was an awesome sight as the cavalry poured over and down the side. The high-pitched sound of the brass bugle accompanied the soldiers like a battle cry as they descended into the fight.

Sergeant Stackhouse hesitated long enough to take a swig from his water flask refilled to the top with whiskey when Lieutenant Halcomb had left to find the woman. It proved his undoing. His horse slipped unsteadily and, instead of being able to pull the reins and bring it back, Stackhouse, his brain too pickled in alcohol to think quickly, lost control. Man and beast went down rolling down the side of the canyon. The horse tumbled, back broken and landed on top of its rider. They went almost unnoticed in the hullabaloo of the charge.

The young Comanche were in time to see the cavalry charging down the walls of the canyon. They had tied the horses carrying the bodies of the dead braves to a log so they could graze but couldn't move too far away. The travois carrying the injured Wolf Slayer was untied and left in the shade.

Broke joined them as they raced down the canyon to the left side of the soldiers. He saw one officer fall from his horse and was saved from using a bullet as the horse fell on top of him. A crushed man wasn't going to get up again. Broke, and the other braves with him, at least had the advantage of being mounted. Other Indians he recognized as Kiowa and Cheyenne, as well as Comanche, were on foot, disorganized and falling like leaves as the soldiers took them by surprise.

Broke didn't see the battle as a conflict with the soldiers: he saw himself trying to prevent the impending slaughter of his friends, their women and children. Shooting Star, Sly Fox, Long Face and One Who Shapes Hunting Tools joined in the fight against the soldiers while Broke defended and helped the women and children to escape.

The soldiers, had they noticed one person out of the thousands in the canyon, wouldn't have recognized Broke as a white man. His year in the wilderness had seen his body bronzed, his hair grown long again and he still wore a breechcloth.

Further along, towards the head of the canyon, he noticed the soldier who'd been instrumental in the loss of Black Horse and the other braves. Lieutenant Halcomb had finally caught up with Colonel Mackenzie's battalions and although not there at the start of the charge, he had sent his men into battle. At the soldier's side, on a horse tethered to his, sat Little Bluestem. Broke didn't wait to see what the others were doing in the battle that raged around him, he focused on the soldier. As far as he was concerned the lieutenant had to pay for the lives he'd taken. He galloped across to them.

'Broke, you're here!'

The lieutenant pulled Little Bluestem's horse closer to him.

'Your friends have not been very successful,' Lieutenant Halcomb said. 'Look, the canyon is cluttered with bodies. They should've done as they were told and avoided all this carnage.'

'And what about the broken treaties?' Broke countered. 'The army hasn't kept its word.'

'Blame the politicians for that. We just follow orders.'

Broke stared at the man. His dismissive manner exasperated him.

'So which politician told you to kidnap this girl?'

Lieutenant Halcomb looked at Broke and then at Little Bluestem and his mouth formed into a sneer.

'Any God-fearing man would've saved the girl from you savages.'

Broke moved his horse to the lieutenant's side and severed the rope that tied Little Bluestem's horse with his knife. He slapped the horse's rump, it took off at a gallop. The lieutenant and Broke faced one another in the middle of the battle.

'You've no one to hide behind now,' Broke said. 'This might be difficult for you but we'll fight man to man.'

The lieutenant's face bleached white then turned red at the insult. His hand went to his Army Colt, but Broke's knife slashed down on his wrist and the gun dropped from his hand. The blood flowed from the cut and soaked into his cuff. Halcomb sought to stop the flow and pinched the folds of skin together, but Broke allowed him no respite and threw himself bodily from his horse to Halcomb's. They fell to the ground and rolled away from beneath the iron-clad hoofs of the horses, finding a patch of land to fight.

'Give me time to bind this cut,' Halcomb pleaded.

Broke had no intention of playing fair, and he didn't trust the lieutenant, not after he'd tricked them into believing he had fewer men than he actually had. It had been a trick that had got Black Horse killed. He vowed to rip off the soldier's scalp as revenge. Wolf Slayer could wear it as a decoration to honour his brother. Halcomb saw the murderous thoughts in Broke's eyes and he didn't bother about rules either, pulling out a derringer from the side of his boot. He moved too late. Broke sailed into Halcomb's chest, and took the wind from the man's body. The weapon dropped to the ground.

However, he was not that easy to beat, because, for all his pomp, Halcomb was a trained fighter. Born with a natural meanness, he was hard to overcome. The loss of blood didn't seem to affect him.

Broke, who'd lived with the Comanche, his body strong and agile, was a match. No sooner than one of them was knocked down, they were on their feet again, fists clenched and ready to strike.

Broke fell upon Halcomb with a vengeance and caught the man with an uppercut to the jaw. He'd found a weak spot. He heard a crunch and followed through with another punch to the chin. Halcomb swayed, dizzy from the blows, red spittle dripping from his lips. Broke took the advantage and threw another punch which smashed Halcomb's nose.

A spray of fine blood covered Broke's chest. He wiped the blood away with the back of his hand. Broke almost admired the man's stamina, but nevertheless was ready to go in for the kill as soon as the opportunity arose. He had also been injured. His body felt inflamed and he reckoned he had cracked a rib as he'd charged into the soldier. Both men were covered with blood, neither certain whose it was.

Although the battle raged around them Broke and Halcomb were now unaware of it as they concentrated on killing each other.

'I reckon you are as welcome on this earth as a rattlesnake at a square dance,' Halcomb spat out the words. 'Everyone will be better off without your kind, you half-breed.'

Broke gave a crooked smile. The soldier knew he

145

was white, but stubbornly refused to acknowledge it. He wondered whether it would always be like this? No place he fitted in?

'And what about Little Bluestem's kind? The one you're "saving" from me. Where does she fit in?'

Halcomb threw a punch while Broke was speaking and shook his fist in pain as it glanced off Broke's strong chin. A wry smile came to his face seeing the split lip. 'It's compensation for the bruised knuckles,' Halcomb said.

They continued to circle one another, breathing laboured as they became exhausted by the effort of the fight. Both seemed to sense they had to finish it before they both fell to the ground. Broke took a beating before he lashed out with a series of devastating blows to Halcomb's body. A blow landed underneath Halcomb's ribs and knocked the breath from his body. The man gasped and groaned, clutched his belly and fell to the ground. He didn't get up. Broke made no checks to see whether the lieutenant was alive or dead. He didn't care. Quickly, he grabbed his knife and scalped the man. He'd vowed to take the scalp to Wolf Slayer as compensation for the murder of Black Horse.

CHAPTER SEVENTEEN

Colonel Mackenzie first hit Chief Lone Wolf's Kiowa camp and routed it.

His information about the place came from his Tonkawa scouts who supplied him with the names of the chiefs and the tribes they led. He believed that the army's success at Palo Duro Canyon could see an end the Indian Wars.

Chief Poor Buffalo and the Cheyenne leader, Iron Shirt, managed to effect some resistance and the Indians retrieved their weapons and advanced towards the soldiers. It was an unequal battle. The soldiers were on horses and most of the Indians were on foot. Heavily armed, the soldiers were too strong for them. The camp, so spread out over the canyon floor, made a unified fight impossible. The Indians' battle was lost before it had begun.

147

The soldiers fired their rifles and brought down the first wave of resistance. Soon the floor of the canyon was covered with corpses, the opposition overcome by the advantage of surprise and superior weapons.

The warriors held their ground for a time, fighting desperately to cover the escape of their squaws and pack animals, but under the persistent fire of the troops they soon began falling back.

This wasn't enough for Colonel Mackenzie who wasn't satisfied with his victory. His orders were to destroy the spirit of the red man. Not cause any more deaths than needed, but to ensure the Indians wouldn't recoup and fight again. He sent men to follow them into the nearby Tule Canyon. There they captured about 2,000 horses. Those horses Mackenzie did not need were slaughtered to prevent them from falling into the Indian's hands. The sound of rifle fire and the agonized screams of 1,500 horses echoed across the canyon and plains.

Another company of soldiers wrecked the villages the Indians had built, burned over 400 lodges, and destroyed countless pounds of buffalo meat.

The look on the warriors' faces summed it up: the loss was devastating. Crushed, they threw down their weapons and surrendered. Although a few stayed to fight on, hiding in the hills and firing at the soldiers, by the day's end it was over. Even if they escaped immediate danger, an Indian band that found itself on foot and out of food generally had no choice but to give up and head for the reservation. An ignoble end to a noble people but surely this way, their leaders told them, they would live to fight another day. Most shook their heads. They couldn't see any way to overcome the scale of the destruction they'd suffered.

By nightfall, the canyon belonged to Colonel Mackenzie and his men.

After the main battle ended Broke looked round for Little Bluestem. She'd escaped from Lieutenant Halcomb only to be recaptured by one of his men. As far as the soldiers from the 4th platoon were concerned she was still a captive. She sat on her horse tethered to Private Hembree's mount. Broke held back from charging towards her, anyone not in an army uniform or civilian clothes risked being shot and yet he knew he had to rescue her. Or at least allow her the chance to say what she wanted to do.

He'd packed his clothes in his saddle-bags before the confrontation with Black Horse. In a fight or a battle, or just to sit and talk to his Indian friends, he preferred to be clothed in their mode of dress. He knew in dealing with the soldiers, or any other white men, he had no choice but to be presentable to them so he put on his jacket, pants and boots, tied his hair back with a strip of leather and placed his bowler hat squarely on his head. Then he spat on his hands and wiped them over his face to rub off the dirt and bloodstains. The lieutenant's scalp he wrapped in his neckerchief and placed in his saddle-bag. He remounted his horse and rode straight towards the man who was in charge.

'Sir,' Broke touched his hat.

Colonel Mackenzie responded with an automatic salute.

'Mister?' he asked. 'What can I do for you?'

'I've come to collect a white woman, Miss Mary Williamston, who lived with the Comanche. She's with that soldier.' He pointed to Private Hembree.

The general looked towards the direction Broke indicated. The area was in chaos. People were running around in confusion everywhere. 'If you want her, take her,' he said. 'Got too many damned Indians around here anyways.'

'Colonel Mackenzie, sir,' Lieutenant Polk of the 11th Infantry interrupted. 'Sergeant Stackhouse of the 4th platoon said Lieutenant Halcomb had gone chasing after a white girl to save her from the clutches of savages.'

'I can't worry about one girl.' General Mackenzie was known for his outspokenness. 'Find Halcomb or Stackhouse or anyone else who knows what's going on and we'll clear the problem up.' He looked at Broke. 'If they don't want her, you can take her. As I said, I've got enough to deal with already.'

A scout was sent to look for the lieutenant. The man galloped back at speed.

'Sir, it seems Lieutenant Halcomb is one of the few soldiers to have suffered injuries. He's barely alive but he's been scalped. Medics are tending to him now. I don't know where Stackhouse, or any other officer from the company, is.'

The general turned round to Broke. 'Looks like you've got the girl,' he said. 'Treat her well.'

'I can assure you of her safety, sir,' Broke replied.

Accompanied by Lieutenant Polk they cantered over to where Little Bluestem sat with Private Hembree.

'Private, you are to release the girl to this man.'

Hembree looked like a child whose candy had just been taken.

'Sir,' he said, 'I have to inform you that he is a half-breed Injun. We rescued her from the Comanche.'

Lieutenant Polk was in no mood to dally. However he couldn't ignore the soldier's concerns. He turned to Broke. 'Is this true?' he asked.

'My name is Mitch Bayfield and my pa owns the Three Bays Ranch in Pecos County, Texas. Mary Williamston did live with the Comanche, but I rescued her.'

'To my ears that don't sound like no half-breed,' Lieutenant Polk said. He turned to the girl. 'You want to go with him?' he asked. 'I got a sister the same age as you back home. Wouldn't want her to be forced into a situation. You're welcome to return to the fort with us and stay with the ladies.'

'I'll be all right, Officer,' she said. 'I've known this man for many years.'

Lieutenant Polk smiled as he took in her soft voice and pretty features underneath the dirt.

'You can't hand her over,' Private Hembree protested. He quailed slightly under the lieutenant's hard stare. 'Sir,' he added.

'Quiet, Soldier,' Lieutenant Polk said. 'Any insubordination will not be tolerated.' With a slight bow of his head towards Little Bluestem and Broke, he ordered Hembree to follow him and they left to rejoin the troops.

Alone, Broke said, 'I'll take you to the Lazy Z Ranch. You'll be able to contact relatives from there. Start over again.'

'I told you I have no one. My folks didn't have any family when they left the East and the raid on our wagon finished everyone off but me. I'll take my chances with you, Broke. That's if you don't mind me tagging along?'

Although it was hard to argue with that, Broke insisted she take some time to rest up. 'You, we, have been through a lot. I'll take you to see Miss Lizbeth.' Little Bluestem's eyes were downcast. 'You'll enjoy meeting her.'

A smile appeared on her face but it was slightly skewed and didn't reach further than her top lip.

Together they went to ride out of Palo Duro Canyon. 'Got one more thing to do before we leave.'

He turned his horse towards where Wolf Slayer and the other braves were. 'I scalped the man who led the attack where my Comanche brothers were wounded or killed.' He took the scalp from his saddle-bag and showed it to her. 'A present,' he said.

'You going to give that to Wolf Slayer?' she asked.

He nodded his head. 'And then I aim to take you to the Lazy Z,' he said.

CHAPTER EIGHTEEN

The meeting with Wolf Slayer was brief. Broke spoke to the injured man as he offered his gift.

'Here is the scalp of the man who led the attack on us. I don't know who shot your brother but this man ordered the charge.'

Wolf Slayer stared fixedly at the bloodied piece of hair before he took it. 'I hope he suffered,' he said.

'Still suffering as far as I know. I didn't check whether I killed him first.'

Wolf Slayer gave a wry grin, which turned into a grimace as any movement pulled at the injury to his chest. He tied the scalp to his belt.

'Thank you for avenging Black Horse,' he said. His eyes were half closed as if to veil his emotions. 'I know this would never have happened if we hadn't followed you. My brother wasn't happy you left our camp. His anger grew when you only came back for that boy. He lost control when you tried to claim a woman he wanted, and you took her.'

'I know he believed I'd made a lot of mistakes.'

'You know nothing about him.' Wolf Slayer's words were flat and cold. 'Because of your obsession with where you and Little Bluestem belong, I have lost a brother.'

Broke recalled the many years they had been together as brothers and friends: growing, playing, hunting and fighting on the northern plains and then, in the latter years, on the reservation by the Red River. Wolf Slayer was now aloof, his face hollow with grief for Black Horse, and deep lines etched into his skin as if to underline the resentment he felt. As Broke watched, the young brave seemed to draw back from the memories they shared together and pushed them from his mind.

At sixteen years he looked like a man of ninety.

'Death is a hard lesson to learn,' Broke said. 'My pain is greater because I have lost two brothers.'

Wolf Slayer didn't argue with him, merely confirmed the end of their friendship as he nodded in agreement.

'I too, have lost two brothers,' he said.

The young Comanche braves collected their dead – Black Horse and Fat Boy and together with the wounded Wolf Slayer and Rider of Horses – and left the canyon. They followed the trail back to the reservation with many other Indians who, after the destruction of Palo Duro Canyon, had nowhere else to go.

Broke and Little Bluestem's journey to the Lazy Z Ranch took a couple of days. There wasn't much conversation between the two riders. It was clear to Broke from Little Bluestem's frostiness that she had nothing to add to what had already been said. Broke didn't try to talk her round as they both accepted that this was something on which they would never agree. Whenever Broke looked in her direction it was as if she was deep in thought. He shrugged his shoulders and rode on silently.

As the Lazy Z Ranch finally came into view, still looking all new and polished like a shiny dollar after its rebuild after the fire, Gil Tander rode out to greet them. 'Good to see you, Broke, and this here young lady. . . .' He paused, pushed his hat back and scratched his head.

'Mary Bluestem,' Little Bluestem said. She turned to Broke. 'I'm not sure where I belong so I'd best take a little bit of both with me.'

'Sounds a pretty name to me,' Tander said. Then he spoke to Broke. 'Crosland Page is home, and he'll be pleased to see you.'

As they stabled the horses and made their way across to the ranch house, Tander explained that Crosland Page gave him more of the responsibility and work to do nowadays.

'The fighting, with your pa and two brothers, and

then finally the fire, took a lot out of him – not that he'd ever admit it – so I help him ease up so he has time to enjoy life.'

When they reached the ranch house Tander knocked at the door, and then opened it as he called out. Broke looked across the room and saw Page sitting in his armchair. He looked as ornery as usual, so nothing had changed, but Broke noticed the hair was greyer and his steps slower than when they last met as he got up and came over to greet them. He still favoured a tailored wool jacket and pants, clothes more suited to a Sunday, and a starched shirt with its collar poking into the loose flesh under his chin.

'So, you finally taking my advice to come home, take over your ranch, and settle down?' His gaze lighted on Little Bluestem as he spoke.

'Not yet,' Broke said.

'You always was a stubborn one,' Crosland Page grumbled.

'I want to ask a favour,' Broke continued.

'Anything, I owe you plenty.'

'Little Bluestem, I mean Mary Bluestem, needs a place for a while. She lived with the Comanche, as I did. I want her to live with a family, like yours, so she can decide what she wants to do.'

Crosland Page looked at the girl whose mouth drooped slightly at the corners. 'I think she's made her mind up already. Nevertheless, Mary, if I can introduce you to Lizbeth, she'd be mighty keen for a woman's help at the moment.'

Broke's expression asked the question.

'No, she's all right. She's in, er, a woman's condition.' Page coloured up. 'Doc reckons it'll be an early summer baby.'

Tander's face had a smile that reached from ear to ear.

'You never mentioned it,' Broke said.

'Weren't the right time,' Tander answered.

Broke nodded.

'Or the fact that Lizbeth was hurt in the robbery?'

'Definitely not the right time, Broke. I would've had to speak up for you again to Marshal Jones. That lawman ain't happy about the number of people you shoot.'

'Never shot anyone who didn't ask to be shot. Still, you got the satisfaction of watching them hang. The trial took place yet?'

Gil Tander looked down as if to examine his boots, and Crosland Page asked Mary if she'd like to wash and rest up before she met Lizbeth. The atmosphere was tense. Finally Tander looked up as if satisfied his boots were shiny enough.

'I see you've got a beautiful palomino out there, Broke. You want to see the latest horses the boys brought in?' he asked.

'You ain't answered my question.'

'Well, the gang escaped. An Injun slipped into the

law office to ask about you, and it seems from what the marshal could tell anyone with his broken skull, the Injun must've thrown them the keys.'

'An' you ain't going after them?'

'That Nixon gang will be far gone by now. They've probably disappeared into New Mexico. An' I got things to do here, what with Lizbeth in her . . . condition.'

'And I don't want him to go, Broke.' Lizbeth looked as if she had an ethereal air about her as she glided into the room. Her face glowed with a beauty impending motherhood bestowed on a woman. She wore a plain blue dress with her swelling waistline partially hidden by a sash that decorated it. 'I saw what anger did to you when you fought with your brother. And I don't want that to happen to Gil.'

Tander was at her side in an instant. 'I ain't going nowhere,' he said. 'Let me introduce you to Broke's friend, Mary Bluestem. She needs a place to stay.'

Lizbeth held her arms open to the girl who had stayed at the edge of the circle of friends.

'What a pretty name you have, Mary Bluestem. Is it because of the colour of your eyes?' Mary nodded and smiled at Lizbeth. 'And if you need a place to stay, I sure need a companion.'

Before Little Bluestem could protest, it seemed to be all settled that she would stay and Broke would go. Before long the two of them stood at the corral together. He saddled his horse and she watched. He looked up after he tightened the saddle straps and saw her forlorn figure. He put his arms around her and held her tightly. His lips found hers and they kissed for a long, long time.

'I haven't forgotten the time we spent together in the cave,' he said.

She blushed.

'Neither have I,' she said. 'You have to go so soon?'

'It's best,' he said. 'It wouldn't be easy living with me 'cause I'm still in no man's land.'

'So where you going?'

'I might head off to New Mexico.'

Little Bluestem knew she couldn't persuade him to stay. He meant to go after the Nixon gang.

'You'll keep in contact with me, letters, I mean?'

Broke laughed. 'It's been a long time since I put words on paper.' He watched her expression turn sad. 'But I think I can make the effort for you.'

The girl watched him ride away from the Lazy Z ranch.

She hoped he wouldn't be gone too long.